Also by Alan Katz

The Day the Mustache Took Over

THE
DAY THE
MUSTACHE
CAME BACK

THE
DAY THE
MUSTACHE
CAME BACK

Alan Katz

illustrations by Kris Easler

BLOOMSBURY
NEW YORK   LONDON   OXFORD   NEW DELHI   SYDNEY

First published in the United States of America in July 2016
by Bloomsbury Children's Books
www.bloomsbury.com

Bloomsbury is a registered trademark of Bloomsbury Publishing Plc

For information about permission to reproduce selections from this book, write to
Permissions, Bloomsbury Children's Books, 1385 Broadway, New York, New York 10018
Bloomsbury books may be purchased for business or promotional use. For information
on bulk purchases please contact Macmillan Corporate and Premium Sales Department at
specialmarkets@macmillan.com

Library of Congress Cataloging-in-Publication Data
Names: Katz, Alan, author.
Title: The day the mustache came back / by Alan Katz.
Description: New York : Bloomsbury Children's Books, 2016.
Summary: When Martin "Murray Poopins" Healey left the Wohlfardt household, all the
responsible habits, good manners, and study skills that twins David and
Nathan had developed under his less-than-watchful eye went out the window,
until Myron, who claims to be Martin's twin, arrives.
Identifiers: LCCN 2015025166
ISBN 978-1-61963-560-9 (hardcover) • ISBN 978-1-61963-561-6 (e-book)
Subjects: | CYAC: Nannies—Fiction. | Behavior—Fiction. | Twins—Fiction. |
Brothers—Fiction. | Humorous stories. | BISAC: JUVENILE FICTION/Humorous Stories. |
JUVENILE FICTION/Family/Siblings. | JUVENILE FICTION/Boys & Men.
Classification: LCC PZ7.K15669 Das 2016 | DDC [Fic]—dc23
LC record available at http://lccn.loc.gov/2015025166

Book design by Amanda Bartlett and Yelena Safronova
Typeset by Newgen Knowledge Works (P) Ltd., Chennai, India
Printed and bound in the U.S.A. by Berryville Graphics Inc., Berryville, Virginia
2 4 6 8 10 9 7 5 3 1

All papers used by Bloomsbury Publishing, Inc., are natural, recyclable products
made from wood grown in well-managed forests. The manufacturing processes
conform to the environmental regulations of the country of origin.

To Nathan and David, the twinniest twins
in the twiniverse

THE
DAY THE
MUSTACHE
CAME BACK

CHAPTER
ONE

The new nanny at the front door said his name was Myron Hyron Dyron. But the way he looked, the way he spoke, even the way he smelled, told twin brothers Nathan and David Wohlfardt that the man standing before them was, in fact, their previous nanny, Martin Healey Discount.

"Martin! You're back!" exclaimed Nathan.

"Yes! You're back!" David said gleefully.

"What do you mean?" asked Myron.

"What do you mean, 'What do you mean?'?" asked David.

"What do you mean, 'What do you mean, what do you mean?'?" asked Myron.

"What do you mean, 'What do you mean, what do you mean, what do you mean?'?" asked Nathan.

"What I mean is my name is Myron. Myron Hyron Dyron. There is certainly no reason to address me as Martin."

"But you *are* Martin," David informed him. "Martin Healey Discount."

"Martin Healey Discount," Nathan added, "who was our nanny for about five months and twenty-nine days!"

"Actually, it was six months. Six months exactly, to the day," Myron said. "But as I said, that wasn't me."

"Oh, come on, Martin, give it up!" Nathan said. "We know it's you! Same face, same out-of-control mustache, same breath . . ."

"Yeah, plus Martin Healey Discount and Myron Hyron Dyron have the same initials.

You look the same, and . . . and . . . and . . . you knew how long Martin lived here before!" David said, as if reciting the charges against a wanted criminal. "So you are you!"

"I am indeed myself," Myron said. "But I am *not* Martin."

"Well, then, you must be twins!" David said.

"That's the first correct thing you've said," answered Myron. "Martin Healey Discount is my twin brother."

"*You're* a twin?" David gasped. "Just like us?"

"Well, not precisely like you," Myron told him. "For one thing, while the two of you live in the same house and are together constantly, such as in your room, at school, and on your recent ski trip, Martin and I have not actually seen each other for fourteen years, three months, and thirty-seven days."

Nathan and David didn't ask why he hadn't said that as fourteen years, four months, and seven days. Not because they weren't curious, but simply because they were both shocked that Myron knew about the ski trip the family had just taken. Also, it frankly never occurred to either one of them that there aren't any months with thirty-seven days.

"That's quite remarkable," Mrs. Wohlfardt said. "You are, in fact, the spitting image of Martin, Myron."

"Including the spit," David whispered to Nathan, having suddenly realized that he was soaked from the way Myron spit a little when he said words starting with *P* or *T* (just as Martin had always done).

"We knew Martin had five brothers and two sisters," Nathan said. "But we never knew he had a twin."

"Ah, I'm sure there are many things about Martin you don't know, little guy," Myron told him.

"Like what?" Nathan wanted to know.

"That's hard to say," Myron said. "Remember,

he and I haven't seen each other in fourteen years, two months, and sixty-seven days."

Again, neither boy questioned Myron's unusual calendar wording.

"Well, any twin of Martin's is a twin of ours, Myron," Mrs. Wohlfardt exclaimed, trying to say that she was glad he was there.

"Thank you, Mrs. Wohlfardt," Myron said.

"It's absolutely wonderful that you're here, Myron," Mrs. Wohlfardt continued, unaware that she was finishing every comment she made to Myron by saying his name—a habit she'd been unable to break whenever she spoke to Martin. "Because since Martin left us, these boys have failed to maintain the organizational skills, study habits, and tidiness that he somehow inspired in them."

"You have my word, Mrs. Wohlfardt, that I will dedicate my days and nights to helping them achieve greatness once again," Myron said, so convincingly that even he believed it.

"Now, if you will excuse me, I will go to my room and unsuit my suitcases, delug my luggage, and distrunkify my trunk."

Nathan and David thought that meant Myron intended to unpack, but they weren't sure . . . until he grabbed his things and headed directly to the room that Martin had previously occupied.

The fact that he knew about the ski trip *and* knew where to go confirmed David's suspicion that this man, who said he was Myron, was, in fact, their previous nanny Martin. Nathan also thought there was an extreme possibility that was true. It was all pretty confusing.

As for Mrs. Wohlfardt, well, she didn't know what to think. Whether it was new Myron or old Martin, she was glad someone was there to watch her boys. And she summed up the whole tricky situation quite well when she said, "My, it's certainly been an interesting eleven minutes and three hundred twenty-seven seconds since he got here!"

CHAPTER
TWO

While the newly arrived (or possibly old and returning) nanny was setting up his room, the boys retreated to theirs—to think, to ponder, to strategize, and to mull things over.

"I know he said he's Myron, but I can't help thinking he's really Martin," David said.

"I'm very surprised," Nathan told him. "Not so much about the whole Myron and Martin thing, but about the fact that you're actually thinking."

"Very nice," David harrumphed. "I think. I think all the time. At least I think I do."

"Look, if Martin was back, why would he bother acting as if he's someone else?" Nathan wondered aloud.

"Based on my just-arrived, new and improved, Double Super-Secret Special Spy Kit and Bad Breath Detector, I have four theories about that," David informed him.

"Let me hear the fourth one, then the second one, then the third one," Nathan said. "And if two out of the three of them make any sense at all, I'll possibly be willing to listen to the first one."

"Okay," David said. "Fourth, Martin could be in some kind of trouble and he's here to hide out from international pickle smugglers."

"No," Nathan said. "Next?"

"Second, Martin could be in some kind of trouble and he's here to hide out from international paper clip smugglers."

"No," Nathan said. "Stop with the trouble and smugglers. And remember, if someone's trying to hide out, they change how they look. He would have shaved his mustache. He would have shaved his head. He totally would not have shown up as his own identical twin!"

David had to admit that was a good point. And since his other two theories both had to do with smuggling (toenail clippers and yellow bouncy balls), he decided not to share them with his brother.

"Then I got nothing," David said. "We're simply gonna have to figure out a way to find out if he's who he says he is, or if he's who we think he might be."

"We could ask him," Nathan suggested.

"No! No, no, no, no, no!" David said. "He insists he's Myron. If we ask him again if he's Martin, that would be insulting."

"We could call the FBI. Then the CIA. Or the IRS. The FCC. The FDA. Or even NASA," Nathan offered.

"Wrong," David said.

Nathan took it further: "Well, how about NBC, CBS, ABC, CNN, and Fox?"

"You're waaaaay off, bro," David told him. "And yet, your extremely rotten ideas have given me a good one."

"Thanks!" Nathan said, beaming with pride.

"See, we need to *be* the FBI, CIA, and all those other governmental investigative agencies. We need to watch this guy like a hawk. We need to monitor his every move. We need to record everything he says and does. We need to be observant. We need to be heedful. We need to be attentive. We need to use his words and actions as evidence that he's Myron . . . or that he's Martin," David said, by now totally breathless.

"Yeah," Nathan answered. "But most of all, there's something else that has to happen right away. . . ."

"What's that?" David asked.

"You need to stop starting all your sentences with 'We need to . . .'"

"Okay," David said. "But one more: as we're investigating the Mysterious Case of Myron or Martin, we need to treat Myron as if he really *is* Myron. We can't assume he's really Martin. We can't call him Martin. We can't act like he's Martin. We can't treat him like we treated Martin. We can't expect him to treat us as Martin did. And we can't—"

"We can't keep starting sentences with 'We can't . . . ,'" Nathan interrupted.

"We can't?" David asked.

"No, we can't," Nathan said.

"What if we need to?" David wanted to know.

"We don't need to. We can't," Nathan insisted.

"Okay," David said.

"Okay," Nathan said.

"Okay," David said.

"Okay," Nathan said.

"Okay," David said.

"Okay," Nathan said.

"Okay," David said.

Nathan wanted to say, "We can't keep saying 'okay,'" but he knew that they'd agreed not to say "We can't . . ." anymore. So this went on for a while. It's probably best if we move on to . . .

CHAPTER THREE

What happens when a new nanny enters your life and acts like your old nanny? Well, it's kind of like switching brands of peanut butter and jelly. It *tastes* like peanut butter and jelly, and it *looks* like peanut butter and jelly, but it probably doesn't taste or look exactly like the peanut butter and jelly you've always known.

When it came to interacting with the man who said he was Myron, Nathan and David immediately recognized the jellyish flavor of his personality. And they sure knew the nutti-ness. It was, in fact, much the same as Martin's brand of nuttiness.

If they were different people, Myron and Martin were clearly nuts from the same family tree. The boys realized all this the very second that Myron rejoined them after having unsuited, delugged, and distrunkified.

David was busy making a Myron or Martin Evidence Chart at the kitchen counter. It looked something like this:

Myron Acts Like Myron	Myron Acts Like Martin	Favorite Types of Pigeons

(The third column was for a school science project that David thought maybe, perhaps, he had due next week. Or last week. Or sometime last year.)

Anyway . . .

David quickly hid the chart as the nanny emerged from his room to address the boys.

"Okay, Nathy and Dathy, here's Myron Hyron Dyron's Fast Five for this morning: it's time to do the dishes, scrub the kitchen floor, alphabetize the soups, dust the telephones—"

"Do the dishes?" David interrupted.

"Scrub the kitchen floor?" Nathan asked.

"Alphabetize the soups?" David asked.

"Dust the telephones?" Nathan asked.

"The fifth item on my list was 'Take a hearing test.' But clearly you've both passed," Myron told them.

"Myron," David said, "your brother Martin *never* made us do chores. Never."

"I believe that is not true," Myron said. "Is it, Nathman?"

Nathan thought about what to say. He didn't exactly want to lie, but he definitely didn't want to do chores. In fact, he wanted no part of Myron Hyron Dyron's Fast Five.

"Welllll," Nathan finally said. "It's not true, but it's also *not* not true."

"It's not?" Myron wanted to know. "Or it's *not* not?"

"Right! It's not not not not!" David explained.

"Not not not not not not!" Nathan added.

But David and Nathan had gone too far. Because after hearing what they'd said, Myron took out a large easel—one the boys had never seen in the house before—and drew what he called his Diagram of Truthfulnessness.

Myron wrote the word "TRUE" on the easel.

"'True,' my friends, means something is true."

The boys nodded in agreement.

Then Myron added the word "NOT" in front of the word "TRUE."

"'Not true,' dear Wohlfardtians, means something is untrue."

The boys nodded in agreement again.

Myron added the words "NOT NOT" in front of the words "NOT TRUE."

"'Not not not true,' little baby boys, means something is not not untrue. And since not untrue is true, not not not true is . . . false."

David gulped hard. *Caught!*

Myron added the words "NOT NOT" in front of the "NOT NOT NOT TRUE" that was already there.

"'Not not not not not true,' you lucky lads, also means you're starting with true, then going to untrue, then back to true, then back to untrue, then back to true, and then back to untrue."

Nathan gulped even harder than David had. *Also caught!*

"So, by that very fact, or as they ought to say in Latin, *ipso fatso*," Myron boomed, "the answer to the question of whether or not Martin made you do chores is . . . yes, without question. Let's begin, and you'll see how chores can be fun!"

Nathan and David both thought about adding "NOT" to Myron's "chores can be fun" statement. But suddenly, they both were extremely confused about how to use that word.

"Before we start, can I ask you one thing?" David asked.

"*May* I ask you one thing," Myron corrected him.

"*May* I ask one thing?" David said, rolling his eyes in a way that he hoped Myron wouldn't notice.

"Yes, you can," Myron said. "What is it, oh child of great curiosity?"

David took a deep breath and said, "Are you *really* gonna make us work around the house? Are you really gonna boss us around? Is there really such a thing as Myron Hyron Dyron's Fast Five? And is it possible to alphabetize the soups, and even if we could, who'd want to?"

"Because that was five questions instead of just one, I will answer all of them, but not necessarily in the order you asked them," Myron said. "So . . . no, yes, people who like to be able to find their soups in a soup emergency, yes, and yes."

Did the boys do all the chores from the list known as Myron Hyron Dyron's Fast Five? Well, let's just say that if you're looking for the Chicken Noodle soup, you'll find it right between the Chicken Gumbo and the Chicken with Rice.

CHAPTER FOUR

"Good morning, Daybreak. Good morning, Night-fall," Myron said to the boys as they sleepily slid into their seats at the breakfast table. "How are you both this bright, sunny Saturday morning?"

"Two things, Myron. First of all," David said. "My name is David, not Daybreak."

"Yeah, and I'm Nathan, not Nightfall," Nathan added.

"You call us everything but our real names!" David complained. "What's up with that?"

"Yeah," Nathan said. "You've been calling us Nathy and Dathy. Nibble and Dibble. Nay-Nay and Day-Day . . ."

David picked up where his brother had trailed off. "Nixon and Dixon. Nipper and Dipper. Even Napkin and Dapkin."

"What's 'Dapkin' even mean?" Nathan said.

"Yeah! And what's a Napk . . . oh, never mind," David said. Though he'd never actually used one, he *did* know what a napkin was.

"Myron, you've been living here as our nanny for more than seventy-one hours now, and we think it's time you called us by our *real* names!" Nathan insisted.

"If you both feel that way, it is certainly not unreasonable of you to ask me to do so," Myron told them. "But first, we must take a vote. And in the true spirit of democracy, it must be a secret ballot. I will turn around and close my eyes; each of you must close your eyes as well."

Myron closed his eyes and turned around to face the wall.

"Okay, let's close our eyes," Myron said.

Though it seemed silly, both boys did as he suggested.

Myron used his important-sounding voice to announce the voting.

"As to the matter of whether or not Myron Hyron Dyron should address the Wohlfardt lads by their birth names, raise your left arm and right leg if you vote yes, and your right arm and left leg to indicate no."

Each boy raised his left arm and right leg. David fell over once, but he got right back up and assumed the "yes" position.

"*Bzzzzz! Bazzzert! Pfiffft!* The official voting period has now concluded," Myron boomed. "You may put your limbs down."

The boys did just that.

"The final vote must now be tallied," Myron told them. "Let's see, two plus seventeen divided by the square root of sixty-four, times eleven plus infinity minus three, carry the fifty-nine. Aha, yes, point six, multiplied by zero . . . and the final results are . . ."

The boys stood there, impatiently waiting for what Myron would say next.

"Sorry, guys," Myron said. "I have no idea how you each voted. See, my eyes were closed and I was facing the other way."

"Myron!" David yelled. "I voted yes!"

"Me too!" Nathan yelled. "Left arm, right leg, yes!"

"The yeses win!" David said. "It's unanimous!"

"Perhaps you mean 'anonymous,' because the voting was unknown," Myron told him. "But actually, now that you've told me how you voted, the balloting wasn't secret, so I'm afraid the vote is negated and disallowed."

The boys were mad. Furious, even.

"Speaking of which," Myron continued, "those are perfectly fine names for you. Negated and Disallowed, please rejoin me at the breakfast table."

Nathan looked into David's eyes. David looked into Nathan's eyes. And perhaps for the first time ever, each twin knew exactly what his brother was thinking about their nanny and their lives.

"I see you looking into each other's eyes with a single thought," Myron said. "My brother Martin and I used to do that—just like two people sharing one brain."

Nathan and David looked at each other again. This time they were both thinking: *if you're two people sharing one brain, chances are your brother Martin has it this week!*

CHAPTER
FIVE

Nathan and David each awoke with a start. They were surprised to see Myron standing between their beds.

"Guys! Guys! It seems as if you both over-slept," Myron told them. "The clock says eight twenty-two a.m., and you're both still snoozing."

"It *can't* be eight twenty-two a.m., Myron!" David insisted. "It's so dark outside."

Nathan would have agreed with David, but he'd already rolled over and fallen back asleep.

"I didn't say it *is* eight twenty-two, young man," Myron told him. "I merely told you that's what the clock says. It is, in fact, five twenty-two a.m."

"But you said we overslept," David protested.

"I didn't actually *say* you overslept. I said *it seems as if* you overslept. It seems that way because I tiptoed in here and set your clock ahead three hours so it would read eight twenty-two and make it seem as if you over-slept," Myron admitted.

"Why did you tiptoe in?" David asked.

"Mommy shoes bowling ball," Nathan said, talking in his sleep during an obviously stranger-than-strange dream.

"I tiptoed in because I didn't want to wake you guys. After all, sleep is really, really, very, really important," Myron informed David.

"Pencil and rice salad so yummy tasty," Nathan said, still dreaming. "More, please, Uncle Pipperman."

"Myron, I wanna go back to sleep. Please . . . ," David said through a yawn as big and wide as the Lincoln Tunnel, which connects Manhattan, New York, and Weehawken, New Jersey.

"Well, who's stopping you?" Myron wanted to know. "In my lifetime, I have been accused of many, many things. I have been accused of causing people to drop their trays of food in cafeterias by simply looking at them. I have been accused of causing twenty-seven-year-old doctors to forget how to swim. I have been accused of having six hundred twenty-nine items in a supermarket line that was meant for shoppers with eight items or less. But I have never, repeat never, repeat never, repeat *never* stopped anyone from sleeping."

"Then don't start now," David told him. "Good night."

"Good night, young da Vinci. Good night," Myron said. "And to help you on your journey to dreamland, I will now sing a song that my mother sang to me when I was a sleepy tadpole of age four, all scrunched up in my bed, wearing my pajamas with a seal wearing pajamas with a snake on them. . . ."

Good night, sleepy tadpole of age four,
All scrunched up in your bed,
Wearing your pajamas with a seal
Wearing pajamas with a snake on them. . . ."

It was a ridiculous song, made even more ridiculous when you consider the fact that David wasn't four and wasn't wearing pajamas showing a seal wearing pajamas with a snake on them. But somehow, Myron's song did the trick. David was quickly sound asleep.

And having heard the song that his mother used to sing, Myron fell asleep too; he was sprawled out on the floor between the boys' beds. In truth, he'd been the one who couldn't sleep, and he only woke them so he'd have the chance to sing—and hear—his favorite lullaby.

If the boys hadn't been asleep, they would most certainly have considered this nighttime interruption the kind of ridiculous thing that Martin would have done, and they would have entered it on the Myron or Martin Evidence Chart, which, by the way, currently looked like this:

Myron Acts Like Myron	Myron Acts Like Martin	Favorite Types of Pigeons
• Calls us other names	• Spits on his letter Ps or Ts • Knew about the ski trip • Knew how long Martin lived here • Tries to trick us • ~~Nathan eats worms~~	• Bokhara Trumpeter

All was quiet in the kids' bedroom at 82727294 Flerch Street in Screamersville, Virginia. Two young lads and their quite unusual live-in nanny were fast asleep, gaining all-important rest and dreaming (what was left of) the night away.

Nathan continued dreaming about Uncle Pipperman's delicious pencil and rice salad.

David dreamed he hit a ninth-inning grand slam to win the final game of the World Series.

And Myron dreamed he made one hundred million dollars as the inventor of edible pants, using the catchy slogan "Everybody deserves a chance to own a pair of edible pants."

All three slept and dreamed happily, until Nathan and David's played-around-with clock struck 10:56 to alert them to the fact that it was 7:56 and time to get up for school.

As for Myron, he slept on the floor until noon. Then he woke up and tried to eat his pants, which, sadly, were corduroy and therefore very hard to digest.

CHAPTER
SIX

It was the time of year when Take Your Kid to Work Day was celebrated, and that meant a huge problem for the boys.

Frankly, both loved their parents equally, but they knew that there were two possibilities: spend the day with their business executive mom at Jordan, Jordan, Jordan, Jordan, and Glerk, where they'd get to sit in on long conferences, hear a never-ending stream of complicated contract terms, and nod a lot . . .

or with their dad, the airline pilot, who would fly them to another city (and then fly right back without doing any sightseeing, though that didn't matter).

Neither boy wanted to miss out on an exciting airline trip.

Yet neither boy wanted to disappoint their mother, of whom they were very proud.

To avoid squabbling, over the past two years Nathan and David had alternated between their parents' jobs. Last year, Nathan went to several twenty-person meetings at J, J, J, J, and G. And David went to Boston. The year before, Nathan went to Chicago. And David went to the bathroom a lot to get out of twenty-person meetings at J, J, J, J, and G.

Based on their turns, this would have been Nathan's year to fly. But David was looking for a way to get on an airplane too, and he had a plan. It was a pretty good plan, because while he had come up with it for purely selfish reasons, it actually appeared to promote brotherly love.

While walking to school, David told his brother, "Here's the deal. We tell Mom and Dad that we want to stay *together* for the visit. We tell them that we will share more and learn more if we both go to the same place. Then, we fly with Dad to California or Florida or somewhere else terrific!"

"What about Mom?" Nathan wanted to know.

"We'll tell her we'll both go with her *next* year," David offered. "And maybe by then, Jordan, Jordan, Jordan, Jordan, and Glerk will have bought a professional sports team, or a rock concert arena, or something else fun."

"It's a *business*, David," Nathan told him. "They don't buy things; they don't have fun. They just have meetings. They talk about contracts, and legal things, and real estate, and lots of other stuff that adults like and kids think is boring."

"Well, then, we'll worry about next year next year," David said.

David thought his plane plan was plain genius (which wouldn't be easy to say, so he didn't say it out loud).

That evening at dinner, the minute Mr. Wohlfardt looked at his boys and uttered his nightly "Hey, you two, what's new?" David cleared his throat and spoke up. Fortunately, he'd rehearsed what he wanted to say so there'd be no chance of anything going wrong.

"Dad, Mom," David said, "Take Your Kid to Work Day is this week, and you both have such interesting jobs. So Nathan and I were thinking: the kid who gets to go with Dad—as I did last year—gets to travel to interesting places."

"Interesting," Nathan said for no apparent reason.

"And," David continued, "while one of us is flying, the other one gets to sit in on meetings and learn all about business, which is absolutely fascinating."

"Interesting," Nathan said again for no apparent reason. "I mean, fascinating."

David ignored his brother and continued: "But if we each go somewhere different, we don't get to *share* the experience. You want us to be close, and so, we think instead of one going with Mom and one going with Dad, we should both go to the same place. And then next year, we'll go together to the other place."

"That's a great idea," Mr. Wohlfardt said.

"A great idea indeed," Mrs. Wohlfardt said.

"Guys, I'm very touched," Myron said as he entered the room with a meat loaf shaped like his head (something his brother Martin had also once served).

"I'm proud of you, boys," Mr. Wohlfardt said.

"I am proud of you, indeed," Mrs. Wohlfardt said. "So where will you go this year?"

"Well, Mom, glad you asked," David said. "Nathan and I were thinking that we'd—"

"Hold it! Hold it! Hold it!" Myron said. "I've got a great idea. Since your mom's place of business name starts with a *J*, and your dad's— Wowie Airlines—starts with a *W* . . . you should go to hers this year, and then you can take a flight together next year."

"Living their lives alphabetically! Brilliant!" Mr. Wohlfardt said.

"Brilliant indeed. Good thinking, Myron," Mrs. Wohlfardt said. "With that simple suggestion, you prevented what could have been a hard decision and a big debate."

But but but but but but but . . . , David thought.

But but but but but but but . . . , Nathan thought.

"So it's settled," Mr. Wohlfardt said. "This Thursday, Nathan and David Wohlfardt will spend nine hours at the conference table at

Jordan, Jordan, Jordan, Jordan, and Glerk! Big business, here they come!"

Nathan and David both smiled weakly.

"And while you're there," Mr. Wohlfardt continued, "I'll be soaring through the skies en route to sunny Puerto Rico!"

"Great plan, Dave," Nathan said mockingly.

"Ugh," David answered, envisioning their dad's plane taking off without them.

Deep down, David couldn't really blame Myron. After all, he knew the nanny was only trying to help.

And even deeper down, he knew that if Myron were actually Martin, it would've somehow turned out that he talked his way into running things at Jordan, Jordan, Jordan, Jordan, and Glerk . . . and then flying to the sunny beaches of Puerto Rico. That was just Martin's way.

Ugh.

Or as his mother would say, "Ugh indeed."

CHAPTER
SEVEN

It was about 144 hours into the days and nights of Myron at the Wohlfardt home.

Although David was happy with the evidence chart he and his brother were keeping, he decided that waiting and watching wasn't good enough; he simply had to step up the investigation in his special master-spy style.

Now, David knew that Myron wouldn't fall for DNA or fingerprinting tactics. He also realized that any attempt to outsmart Myron was doomed to fail. He considered telling the nanny that he was writing a school essay on his favorite person, and since he'd picked Myron, he needed to ask him 148 important questions. But David also knew that Myron would see right through that approach. And besides, who wanted to write a school essay for no reason?

No, David realized, to truly get at the heart of the man with the triple-rhyming name, he'd have to resort to something he'd rarely tried:

The truth.

David picked an afternoon when he knew Nathan wouldn't be around. On that afternoon, Nathan had cartooning club practice or soccer practice or some other practice. David wasn't really sure where Nathan was, because he didn't really pay attention to what his brother was doing—he just knew there was something Nathan definitely needed to practice, and he was just glad his brother was nowhere in sight.

Myron, sitting on a kitchen stool, was extremely busy trying to look extremely busy—though on close examination, he wasn't actually doing anything productive. In fact, he was using bananas to try to peel potatoes, which is pretty much what Martin used to do . . . just the other way around.

"Hey, Mylo," David said to him. "Time for you and me to have a little chat."

"How little?" the nanny wanted to know.

"Well, not really little at all," David admitted. "Medium. Big. Huge. Gigantic."

"What's on your mind, Dancerman?" Myron responded.

David took a deep breath and, speaking faster than he meant to, but not as fast as the time years ago when he had to explain to Ibi, a former nanny, why he'd squirted a whole bottle of chocolate syrup into his mouth at four o'clock in the morning, blurted out, "Well, when you got here, we were pretty sure that you weren't Myron, but were actually Martin. We thought that for some reason you were saying you were Myron, but that you were really Martin. Not Myron, but Martin, coming back to the family."

Myron held up one finger.

"Bathroom break. I'll be right back," he said.

Myron scampered away. David waited and collected his thoughts.

When Myron returned, he said, "Sorry, really had to go. But I didn't wash my hands, so I could get back to you sooner. Please continue, won't you?"

"Um," David continued, "you explained to us that Martin was your twin, and that made sense, so we accepted it."

"Yes, good. Listen, when it came to kids, my mother

got a buy one, get one free special. Just like yours did," Myron said.

"Yeah, but . . . ," David said.

"You had Martin for a while; now you've got me," Myron said. "So what's the problemomomo?"

"As we've gotten to know you, we've seen that you really do look like Martin. You act like him. You talk like him. You dress like him. You snore like him. You treat us just as he did. And you know things only he could know, like how many months he was here and where in the house his bedroom was. So we've come to the conclusion that you must *be* Martin," David said.

"What if I am?" Myron wanted to know.

"Are you?" David asked.

"Am I what?" Myron asked.

"Martin?"

"No."

"Myron?"

"Yes."

"Are you sure?"

"Are *you* sure?"

"No."

"Are *you* Martin?"

"No."

"Nathan?"

"No."

"Fred?"

"Who's Fred?

"I don't know. Are you David?"

"Yes."

"Good. Now we know each other's name. I'm glad that's over."

"Wait, Myron," David continued. "Why do you have a different *last* name than your twin?"

"Why do you have the *same* last name as yours?"

"We just do."

"Well, we just don't."

"It's very suspicious."

"Why would my having a different last name than my twin make you suspicious?"

"I don't know; it just does."

"Okay, I'll say it one more time. Listen carefully: I am Myron Hyron Dyron. My twin brother is Martin Healey Discount, who apparently looks like me, acts like me, and talks like me, dresses and snores like me, but is a totally different person than I am. I have two eyeballs. He has two other eyeballs. I have a tongue. He has a different tongue. I have a spleen. He has his own spleen. Get it? Got it? Good. And thank you for playing America's favorite game show, *So You Think Myron Is Martin?*"

David shrugged and started to walk away.

"Wait, I do have one thing to say. Something that's hard to admit, but something I must tell you at this time," Myron said.

"Yes, Myron? Yes?" David said excitedly. "What? What? What what what? Tell me!"

"I haven't blown my nose in seven weeks. But I plan to sometime later today."

"Good luck with that," David said, leaving the room not knowing anything more than he did before.

So much for trying to find something out by using the truth, David thought. *I'll never try that again.*

CHAPTER EIGHT

David pulled Nathan into the family's coat closet so he could secretly tell Nathan the whole story about the conversation he'd had with Martin. Sitting there in the dark, he spoke in hushed tones, and admitted to being pretty frustrated.

"Good try, I guess," Nathan said. "But look, it's possible we'll never find out if Myron is really Myron. And ya know what? Maybe it doesn't matter."

"How could you ever say it doesn't matter?" David said, louder than he'd meant to. "It matters."

"Why?"

"Because it matters. It just does," David said.

"That's ridiculous!" Nathan yelled.

"What's ridiculous?" Myron wanted to know as he opened the closet and stepped inside to join the boys in the dark. "Why are you yelling? And most of all, why are you boys sitting in the closet?"

"Um, er, we're planning a surprise party for your birthday!" Nathan said.

"Don't make me laugh!" Myron said. "My birthday's not until the thirty-first, and you guys never plan anything this far in advance."

"Gee, well . . . ," David stammered.

"Listen, guys, whatever you're doing, this is a totally weird place to be doing it. The only time you'll ever catch me sitting in a dark closet is when I overhear my sports coat and parka fighting with each other and I have to step in and settle things. Or sometimes if I'm practicing my harmonica and don't want to give the houseplants a headache. Other-wise, this is not the place to be, guys," Myron scolded.

The boys laughed nervously and told him they were almost done.

"Now, if you'll excuse me," Myron said, "I have to go wash the windows with lemony tuna salad. Good-bye."

With that, Myron slipped out of the closet and closed the door again.

Nathan and David remained in the dark, sweating, both because it was hot and because they'd just collected some very valuable evidence.

"He hears his clothes fighting! That's totally something Martin would do!" David whispered.

"He's afraid of bothering the houseplants with harmonica playing! That also sounds like a Martin thing!" Nathan whispered.

"He washes the windows with lemony tuna salad! Martin actually did that!" David whispered.

"And his birthday is on the thirty-first! Same date as Martin's!" Nathan whispered.

"How do you know Martin's birthday?" David whispered back.

"Because he always told me that he was born two days before the thirty-third," Nathan replied.

"So yeah, the thirty-first! Though *that's* not so surprising—twins usually *do* have the same birthday," David told him.

"Oh yeah," Nathan said. "Remind me to wish you a happy birthday on my next one."

"So . . . I think when you add it all up, we've proven that Myron is indeed Martin," David said.

"Or . . . perhaps there's never been a Martin at all, and it was Myron who was here before and he's back again now?" Nathan suggested.

"Oooh, spooky," David said.

"Yeah, spooky," Nathan said.

Even the sports coat and parka hanging beside them had to agree there was something spooky going on in the Wohlfardt house.

CHAPTER
NINE

The following Saturday, Myron picked up his cell phone on the first ring, cleared his throat, and said, "Thank you for calling the Myron Hyron Dyron Yard Cleaner-Upper Service, home of the 'rake 'em and take 'em' lifetime warranty. Sorry we can't speak to you right now, but we are busy giving someone else's property a pre-spring cleanup. Ah, pre-spring, my favorite pre-season of the pre-year! Any-hoo, please leave a message at the sound of the beep, and one of our caring lawn care special-ists will return your call promptly."

Then Myron made a sound like a beep . . . and listened for a little while before hanging up.

Nathan and David, standing nearby, slapped their foreheads at the exact same time. They both knew that *they* were the "we" Myron had men-tioned. They both knew that Myron was planning to have them be the yard cleaner-uppers. And they both knew this wouldn't be a good day.

"Hey, Myron!" David yelled. "I'm not raking."

"Hey, Myron!" Nathan yelled. "I'm not rak-ing either."

"I didn't ask you to rake," Myron responded. "But more importantly, let's discuss the fact that I also did not ask you to listen to my private telephone call."

Nathan told Myron that it was hardly a pri-vate call, since he'd answered it right in front of them. He did have one question, though.

"Why did you act like you were an answering machine?" Nathan wanted to know.

"My voice mail hasn't been working since I dropped this phone in a boiling pot of chili a week ago Thursday. No, Tuesday. No, Thursday. No, Tuesday," Myron told him. "So I have to act like I'm a recording, beep like voice mail would, and then listen to the message that the caller thinks she's leaving."

"Wait—why didn't you just answer the call and actually talk to the person?" Nathan asked.

"Never thought of that, kid. Never thought of that," Myron said. "Though I suppose that's what a caring lawn care specialist should do."

"I got a question too, Myron," David said. "What's a 'rake 'em and take 'em' lifetime warranty?"

"Simple," Myron said. "Once the leaves, sticks, and twigs are raked and taked . . . er, raken and taken . . . um, raked and taken, we promise that they are gone for good."

"But, Myron," David said, "if the trees are still there, how can you be sure leaves and sticks and twigs will never fall on that lawn again?"

"Of course there'll be *other* leaves and stuff, silly," Myron told him. "But we promise that *what we take away* won't ever return."

"Mighty impressive," David told him, not meaning it.

"Truly outstanding," Nathan added, also not meaning it. "Especially since this is the time of year when there are hardly any leaves on the ground."

"Nukey, Dukey, remember that it isn't how many leaves there are on a lawn that matters," Myron told them. "It's how many there *aren't*. Understand?"

"No."

"No."

"Terrific. After the Myron Hyron Dyron Yard Cleaner-Upper Service does its job, the home-owner will spot a spotless lawn. And best of all, you boys never have to worry about picking up a rake," Myron said, definitely not meaning it.

"That's good," said David. "Because if your brother Martin were doing this"—*and we're not so sure he's not,* David thought—"it's a solid bet that we'd be doing all the work and he'd be getting all the glory."

"Right," Nathan agreed. "He'd have us rake for four hundred and twelve hours without a break, then make us count everything by hand so he could charge per leaf, stick, or twig."

"I don't like what you're saying about my dear brother," Myron said. "And most of all, I don't like pepper-and-onion sandwiches. But as I said, you never have to worry about picking up a rake. No, sir. No way. No chance."

"Good," David told him.

"Good," Nathan told him.

Myron continued, "As the individual in charge of your care, it would be wrong of me to suggest that you help me do a pre-spring cleanup at another family's house, even if it meant that my back—already sore from hours of needless bongo drumming as a youth— might then ache for days, weeks, and even hours thereafter."

"Good," David told him.

"Good," Nathan told him.

"It would be wrong of me to suggest that you give up your free time to assist the one person who is currently devoting his entire life to your welfare," Myron said in a highly dramatic voice.

"Good," David told him.

"Good," Nathan told him.

"And most of all," Myron said, "it would be wrong of me to allow you to use the Rake-tronic 6750 Power Rake, my first and greatest invention—"

"How can it be the first *and* the greatest?" David wanted to know.

"It is the first because I haven't invented anything before this," Myron informed him. "And it is the greatest because in the future, I fully intend to invent a whole bunch of stuff that won't be anywhere near as good."

Oddly enough, that made sense to the boys. But what *didn't* make sense to them was why

Myron didn't want them to use the Rake-tronic 6750.

"Gee, Myron," Nathan said. "You've got a new invention and we can't try it?"

"Don't you trust us, Myron?" David added.

"It's not that I don't trust you," Myron told them. "In fact, I *don't* don't trust you. It's just that it would be wrong of me to have you use the Rake-tronic 6750, because I promised you you'd never have to worry about picking up a rake. And a broken promise is a promise broken."

David and Nathan tried to convince Myron that technically, they wouldn't be picking up a rake—they'd be picking up a power rake. Therefore, Myron wouldn't be breaking a promise; he'd be *power*-breaking a promise. And they pointed out that furthermore, a pre-spring cleanup shouldn't be a hard job, since there weren't as many leaves, sticks, and twigs as there were in other seasons. All they'd have to do is take care of what had collected on the lawn over the winter.

The boys must have done a good job convincing him, because fourteen seconds later, they were booked to spend the whole next day cleaning up yards all over Screamersville.

CHAPTER
TEN

"I have one question, Myron," David said as they arrived at the first lawn. "If you're our full-time nanny, how is it okay for you to also have a lawn care business?"

"Kid, the way I see it, it's all about hobbies. Some people use their spare time to sing opera. Others collect coins or stamps, or create interesting artwork out of dryer lint. Me, I like lawn care. I much prefer the great outdoors to the semi-great indoors."

"So our parents *don't* know anything about it, Myron?" Nathan asked.

"Other kid, when your mom and dad were interviewing me for the nanny job, they asked if I had any hobbies, and I said, 'Yes, I like to dabble in lawn care.' Then, while your father kept talking about how it'd been a long time since he'd heard anyone use the word 'dabble,' I told your mother that I enjoy the science of lawn care, that sometimes I like to assist neighbors with their lawns, and that I donate all profits to help the lawnless."

Neither boy questioned the ridiculous notion of helping the lawnless, or pointed out that, in fact, the lawnless wouldn't need help when it came to lawn care. They both had more to ask about the whole business of their nanny having such a business.

"Do our parents know about the Rake-tronic 6750 Power Rake?" Nathan asked.

"Well, I told them that I like to dabble in inventing," Myron said. "And your father remarked that it'd been a long time since he'd heard anyone use the word 'dabble'—and that now he'd heard it twice in a matter of minutes. Meanwhile, your mother and I discussed the Rake-tronic 6750. She thought it was an excellent idea."

"She did?" David wanted to know.

"Sure she did," Myron insisted. "See, based on my highly calculated calculations, an ordinary rake can handle 1,735 leaves per minute. And since you both know that the average tree releases an average of 142,270 leaves, that would take a raker using an ordinary rake 82 minutes to collect."

"Are those actual numbers?" Nathan asked.

"Indeed they *are* actual numbers," Myron said. "They might not, however, be the correct numbers. Carrying on, I said that collecting those 142,270 leaves would take 82 minutes the old-fashioned way, right?"

"Right."

"Right."

"Well," Myron said. "Prepare to gasp, because the Rake-tronic 6750 Power Rake can handle the same tough job not in 82 minutes, not in 57.45 minutes, not in 28.89 minutes, but in a shockingly short, astoundingly abbreviated 117 seconds! It also sucks up sticks and takes away twigs faster than the human eye can see."

"That can't be true," David said.

Nathan agreed with his brother.

"Laugh if you want to, Nonbeliever and Disbeliever," Myron told them. "But your mother was wildly impressed that in actual field testing, conducted in an actual field, those were the results delivered by the Rake-tronic 6750. Of course, your outcome may vary based on the temperature, the wind speed, the size of the lawn, the placement and the colorfulness of the leaves, the middle name of the homeowner, and fifteen or sixteen other factors."

"So basically we wouldn't save any time by using the Rake-tronic 6750?" David asked.

"Basically, none at all," Myron admitted. "Especially since the man who did the field testing for me is a tremendous liar."

CHAPTER
ELEVEN

Myron had led Nathan and David to the Clark family's leaf-filled lawn, where it took the boys about an hour to set up the Rake-tronic 6750. Myron supervised as they assembled and attached dozens of confusing wires and random parts.

"No, no, David," Myron said at a particularly troubling moment of put-togethering. "You can't attach confusing wire number 17 to random part number 88 until after it's been connected to confusing wire number 363! If you skip that step, the congrogler won't mepulate when you press the paficator!"

Congrogler? Mepulate? Paficator? Nathan and David had never heard of those words. In fact, *no* one had ever heard of those words. But they kept putting the contraption together under Myron's watchful eye (while his other eye, the non-watchful one, dozed off from time to time).

When they were all done, they had a giant device that looked like a broom with an electric juicer near the top, a shoe buffer near the middle, and a waffle iron where the raking prongs would typically be. In fact, that's exactly what it was.

"Okay, let's turn this thing on, grab all the leaves in 117 seconds, and get out of here!" Nathan declared.

"Hit the button marked 'power,'" David added. "And by the way, watch your spelling,

Myron! You wrote 'power' with the *w* before the *o* . . ."

"Wait, wait, hold it! Hold it, wait, wait!" Myron insisted. "Neither of you has an official town license to operate the Rake-tronic 6750!"

"A license? How can the town give a license for something that's never existed before?" Nathan asked.

"What am I, the mayor?" Myron asked. "Which reminds me, remind me to run for mayor. Or governor. And listen, the sad fact is that according to official town code 7–101B, and I quote, 'No Screamersville resident may power up a motorized device designed to clean up a lawn on a Sunday, Thursday, or Friday in May, August, or September unless a permit has first been acquired. Furthermore, permits are only issued on Sundays, Mondays, and Wednesdays in January, February, and October, unless otherwise indicated in official town code 7–101C, which also states that horizontal stripes may not be worn vertically.' "

"I don't get it," said Nathan.

"I don't get it either," said David.

"What it means, my dear Nippippity and Dippippity, is that it appears you cannot use this miracle of leafular engineering," Myron said.

"Well, then, you'll have to do all the work," David said.

"Yeah, right," Myron giggled. "I mean, unfortunately, I don't have a permit either. So we have two choices: One, we can wait until October and get an official town permit. Or two, we can skip the whole thing and leave the leaves."

"Either way, let's go home," Nathan said.

Myron brightened. "Of course, there is a third choice we could pursue. But no, no, I think not. Well, perhaps. Oh, I think not. Then again . . ."

Nathan waited.

David waited.

Nathan finally asked, "What's the third choice, Myron?"

"It'd better not be 'You boys can rake the whole yard while I watch,' " David added.

"That is not at all the third choice, sir," Myron scolded him. "But this is: The official town code says we can't 'power up' a device. But the button on the Rake-tronic 6750 says 'pwoer'—so we'd be 'pwoering' it up." There's no law against that!"

"Are you sure?" asked Nathan.

"Doesn't really seem right," added David.

"Listen, guys. Though I'm not a legal expert, I've watched over two thousand call-a-lawyer commercials, and I was once almost in the same town as some famous TV judge on a show where people sue each other over missing shoelaces or lost pet ladybugs. Well, it was some famous TV judge's friend's niece.

But still, I know that power and pwoer are two very different things. Pwoer to the People!" exclaimed Myron, spitting quite a bit on the *P*s.

"Maybe it should be 'Pwoer to the Poeple,'" said Nathan.

"Indeed," said Myron. "Here goes . . ."

They all closed their eyes as Myron pressed the button.

The Rake-tronic blurped and fizzled and sizzled. You might even say it sneezed and coughed.

"I smell waffles," David said.

"I smell freshly squeezed juice," Nathan said.

"I smell disaster," Myron said. "Ruuuuuuun!"

The good news is that Myron, Nathan, and David were far, far away by the time the Rake-tronic 6750 blew up.

The bad news, however, is that when the Rake-tronic 6750 blew up, it scattered 6,750 teeny-tiny pieces all over the Clark family's yard.

The further bad news, however, is that the boys and Myron (but mostly the boys) had to pick up all 6,750 teeny-tiny pieces. And while they were doing that, Myron suggested that they (again, mostly the boys) rake up all the leaves, sticks, and twigs in the yard. When they finished, the Clarks had the cleanest yard in town, thanks to the Myron Hyron Dyron Yard Cleaner-Upper

Service's "rake 'em and take 'em" lifetime warranty.

That was also good news. For the Clarks.

But it was the worst possible news for Nathan and David and Myron. Because as it turned out, the call for a pre-spring cleanup hadn't come from the Clarks at all. See, Myron thought he'd heard "Mr. Clark," but the person who'd called was actually Mrs. Majawaja-howitz, who lived three houses down from the Clarks.

Mr. Clark refused to pay a penny for the cleanup, though he did say thank you and invite them to come back in the fall and do the job again.

CHAPTER TWELVE

It had been twenty days and thirty-one hours since Myron had joined the family. And since it was the first Tuesday of the month, it was his night off. That's why Nathan, David, and their parents found themselves having dinner at Too-Much Charlie's, Home of the All-You-Can-Eat Salad, Bread, Entrée, Dessert, and After-Dinner-Mint Bar.

David was happily dipping his cotton candy into his shrimp cocktail supreme when his

father cleared his throat and said in a very serious tone, "Boys, we need to talk about Myron."

"Yes, boys," Mrs. Wohlfardt echoed. "We need to talk about Myron."

"Is there something wrong, Mom and Dad?" Nathan asked. "Is he leaving?"

"No, he's not leaving, Nathan. At least, not as far as we know," Mr. Wohlfardt said, fully aware that the family was pretty terrible at predicting when a nanny might depart. "But your mother and I want to have a family discussion about how Myron is doing, and how you are doing with him."

"See, boys," their mother said, "in business, it's often a good idea to review a situation, to see if everything is operating as it should. Sometimes such an investigation can lead to better sales and increased progress."

"Of course, we know that you guys aren't actually selling anything," their dad added. "But in your case, an open conversation could lead to making you happier and more responsible. It could also improve your grades, and add to your overall well-being."

"It could even make Myron more contented and glad to be with us," their mother said, smiling.

"So let's chat," Mr. Wohlfardt said. "How is Myron doing?"

"Good," Nathan said.

"Good," David said.

"Let's be more specific," Mr. Wohlfardt suggested. "For example, how is Myron in terms of helping you with school?"

"Good," David said.

"Good," Nathan said.

"How about we think about things by comparison?" Mrs. Wohlfardt said. "When it comes to helping you with school matters, would you say Myron is better or not as good as Martin, your last nanny, was?"

"Better," Nathan said.

"Butter," David said.

Nathan and his parents looked at David.

"What? I want someone to pass the butter," David explained.

Mrs. Wohlfardt gave her son the butter. And she stared at him until he answered the question about Martin vs. Myron.

"Martin was helpful, and so is Myron," David said. "But it's usually the kind of help where you have to figure out *why* it's helpful."

"What do you mean?" his dad wanted to know.

"Like, when there's math homework, most of our other nannies would lead us to the right answer. Myron helps us get to the wrong answer, but he tells us it's the wrong answer, so we keep going to find the right one," David said.

Nathan continued the thought: "You basically have to take small pieces of Myron's advice. You can't just consider—"

"The whole enchilada," David interrupted.

There was a pause until David added, "What? I want someone to pass the whole enchilada that I brought from the buffet that somehow got moved to the other side of the table."

Nathan slammed the enchilada plate down near David and said: "Yeah, Myron can be tricky. But if you know he's tricking you, you can always out-trick him."

"Unless he knows you're gonna out-trick him. Then you have to watch for him to be straightforward without any tricks at all," David warned.

"Myron also challenges us when it comes to meals, tidying up, even—"

"Dressing," David interrupted.

Mr. Wohlfardt scowled and pushed the dressing toward David.

"No, I wasn't asking for the salad dressing. I mean, he tricks us when we're dressing for school. He tells us to dress sloppily so that we dress neat. He pretty much makes our whole lives one big brain teaser," David said.

"The main thing is, if we figure out what he's really trying to say, we learn," Nathan said.

"Interesting approach," Mr. Wohlfardt said, stroking his face to feel a beard that he actually hadn't had in more than ten years.

"I think it's based on the Backwardian theory of knowledge," said Mrs. Wohlfardt, stroking her chin, where, of course, she'd never had a beard.

"Really, Myron is almost exactly the same as Martin was. In pretty much every way," David said.

"Do you agree with David?" Mr. Wohlfardt asked Nathan.

"Agreeing with that squirrel is bad for my reputation," Nathan said. "But Myron and

Martin are extremely alike. In fact, there are times when Myron says or does something and it reminds me so much of Martin . . . that I'm pretty sure *they are actually the same person!*"

"We've been keeping a list of differences and similarities," David told them, taking out the extremely messy, extremely crumpled Myron or Martin Evidence Chart.

Myron Acts Like Myron	Myron Acts Like Martin	Favorite Types of Pigeons
• Calls us other names • Flosses 812 times a day • Didn't try to get in on Take Your Kid to Work Day	• Spits on his letter *P*s or *T*s • Knew about the ski trip • Knew how long Martin lived here • Tries to trick us	• Bokhara Trumpeter • Bohemian Fairy Swallow

Myron Acts Like Myron	Myron Acts Like Martin	Favorite Types of Pigeons
• Hears clothes fighting • Thinks harmonica playing bothers plants • "Invented" Rake-tronic 6750	• ~~Nathan eats worms~~ • Makes meat loaf shaped like head • Washes windows with lemony tuna • ~~Gets us to do his work~~ • Sleeps when he should be working • Sleeps when he should be sleeping	

"This is very interesting," Mrs. Wohlfardt said, carefully studying the chart. "Very interesting indeed. And tremendously eye-opening."

"What does it say?" Mr. Wohlfardt wanted to know.

"According to this chart," she told him, "the Bohemian Fairy Swallow is a pigeon. I always thought it was a swallow."

"I did too," Mr. Wohlfardt admitted.

"Check, please," David said, slapping his forehead. And his brother.

CHAPTER
THIRTEEN

A few days later, while Nathan was at practice practice, David and Myron were alone in the house.

"Hey, do you want to take a walk with me to the library, oh great Dictionarian?" Myron wanted to know. "I have a book about returning library books to return."

"No thanks, Mart—I mean, Myron," David said, slipping on the nanny's name, since evidence and conversations had been making him more suspicious than ever that Myron, in fact, was Martin.

"Okay, I'll be back before you can say, 'Hello, glad to see you back here so soon'!" Myron told him.

With that, Myron walked out. David stood alone in the kitchen, swirling and curling interesting designs in the banana-and-potato stains that Myron had mashed into the counter quite a long time ago.

Less than ten seconds had gone by since Myron had left for the library, so David was somewhat surprised when he saw a mustache— and the man attached to it—walk into the house.

"Hello, glad to see you back here so soon." David laughed. "Forget something? Like your book, or your wallet, or your eyeballs, tongue, or spleen, perhaps?"

"Is that any way to say hello to your all-time favorite nanny?" the man asked.

Not noticing that the nanny was wearing a red coat instead of the blue one he'd seen just a moment before, David laughed and decided he would play along.

"Oh, how I've missed you since you left!" David said. "The pain, the agony, the longing and hoping that you'd someday return!"

David ran across the room and gave him a giant hug.

"That's better," was the nanny's response.

"Life was so hard without you," David continued. "And even though you were only gone for maybe ten seconds, it felt like months and months and months!"

"Ten seconds? What do you mean?" asked the nanny.

"What do you mean, 'What do you mean?'?" asked David.

"What do you mean, 'What do you mean, what do you mean?'?" asked the nanny.

"Can we please not do this again?" asked David.

"What do you mean, 'again'?" the nanny wanted to know.

"We had a whole 'what do you mean, what do you mean' conversation on the day you got here," David said.

"No, we didn't."

"Yes, we did."

"You got taller since I saw you," the nanny said. "How's school?

"Yeah, right," David scoffed. "Good one, Myron."

"Myron? *Myron?* Gee, did I ever tell you about my brother Myron?" the man wanted to know. "How odd. I simply don't remember doing that."

"Stop it, Myron," David said.

"I'm not Myron, I'm Martin," the man said.

"Stop it, Myron," David said. "It was funny once, but—"

"I tell you, *I am Martin*," the man insisted. "Myron is my long-lost twin brother."

"I don't believe any of this!" David said.

"Don't believe any of what?" Nathan asked as he walked into the house wearing his soccer uniform—even though he was coming from cartooning club practice.

"Your brother doesn't believe that I am none other than Martin Healey Discount," the man who insisted he was Martin told the boys.

"Wait, I'm confused," Nathan said.

"Well, *I'm* confused that you're confused," the man replied.

"You being confused about his confusion is confusing to me," David said.

"You've got to believe me. It's me, Martin. How can I convince you, Nathan and David?" the man wanted to know.

"You just did," Nathan said, with a touch of surprise in his voice. "When you called us Nathan and David."

"Yep, I'm convinced too," David agreed. "Because Myron *never* calls us by our real names."

"Right," added Nathan. "But you did, right off the bat. Which means you are, without question, Martin."

"Well, welcome back to me, then," Martin said. "Now it's time for you to show me that it's so good to see me!"

The boys rushed to Martin and gave him a seventeen-second hug, which is pretty much the longest hug either of them had ever given anyone, if you don't count the time Aunt Selma surprised them each with one hundred dollars cash for their birthday. Technically, her hug lasted twenty-four seconds, but it involved two hundred dollars cash, so really the seventeen-second "free" hug was much more impressive.

"Where have you been, Martin?" David wanted to know.

"Yeah," Nathan added. "And why are you back?"

Martin struck a pose and delivered a speech. "Nathan, that sounds like you don't *want* me back. But of course, that could not be the case.

You simply misspoke. Or perhaps I misheard. Perhaps it is a combination of both. At any rate, I have returned because although travels through exotic lands are, well, exotic, and while it's wonderful to live where fresh, ripe papaya freely walk the streets, the truth is . . . I missed you numbskulls."

"We've missed you too, Martin," David said. "After you left us, things got pretty terrible around here. We fought a lot. We couldn't concentrate on schoolwork. Our room turned into a sloppy pigsty again. We kind of went back to being the horrible kids we were before you ever showed up."

"The kid's right, Martin," Nathan added. "Although he was far horribler."

David ignored this, and continued: "Most of all, our mom and dad were totally frantic without the best kid-watcher in the world in the house."

"Aw, thanks, kid," Martin said. "But the big news is that all the horribleosity is over and you don't have to live without a nanny any longer—Martin Healey Discount is back, and he's back on the job!"

David slid over next to Nathan and whispered into his ear.

"You better tell him about Myron."

Nathan scowled and whispered back.

"*You* better tell him about Myron."

"No, *you*."

"No, *you*."

"I can't tell him that."

"Well, *I* can't tell him that."

Now, Martin may not have been the brightest man in the world, but he knew something was up. He replayed the last few minutes of conversation in his mind, finally put two and two together, and said, "Uh-oh, guys. I get the sense that one of two insane things is happening. If I'm thinking this through correctly, either your mother has a Top 40 country hit called 'You Better Tell Him About Myron' or . . . my twin brother is living with the Wohlfardt family, doing *my* job!"

The boys were somewhat impressed by Martin's reasoning skills.

"Guys, it's as plain as the noses on your faces," Martin said, his lip quivering. "I can tell in your four eyes which of my guesses is correct, and frankly, it's, it's, it's my worst nightmare come true."

"I'm afraid so, Martin," Nathan said.

"Yeah, tough break," David added.

Martin blubbered as he said, "I simply cannot, cannot, cannot believe that your mother achieved country music stardom before I ever could!"

And with that, Martin stormed out.

CHAPTER
FOURTEEN

David looked at Nathan. Nathan looked at David. David looked back. Then Nathan did the same.

Somehow, what had just happened was too much for their young minds to process. Even the fact that combined they technically had the mental brainpower of someone who was practically an adult didn't make it any easier to understand.

"Let's review," David said slowly. "Martin Healey Discount stopped being our nanny, so Mom and Dad hired Myron Hyron Dyron. Myron Hyron Dyron becomes our nanny, and he goes out, and in walks Martin Healey Discount, who's come back to be our nanny. But . . ."

". . . Martin Healey Discount doesn't know that Myron Hyron Dyron is now our nanny . . . ," Nathan continued.

". . . and Myron Hyron Dyron doesn't know that . . ."

"Myron Hyron Dyron doesn't know *what*?" the man said as he walked through the front door.

Neither boy noticed that this man was wearing a blue coat instead of the one they'd just seen. If they had, perhaps they would have come to the conclusion that it was Myron, back from the library.

But alas, that conclusion would have been . . . wrong. It was Martin again; he'd gone outside, changed his coat to the warmer one he always kept hidden deep in the front bushes, and come back inside.

"M-Myron?" David asked, tentatively, still not knowing.

"M-M-Myron?" Nathan asked, even more tentatively (which you can tell by the extra *M* he added to the name).

"Guys, I told you—I'm Martin. Martin. M-A-R-T, um. I'm pretty sure there's more letters, but I always forget which ones," Martin said. "Anyway, men, stop talking about my brother Myron!"

"This is like one of those books where one person walks out the door, and his look-alike walks in, and the people in the room don't know who's who," Nathan said.

"Yeah, like *The Parent Trap*," David said.

"You never read *The Parent Trap*," Nathan told him.

"No, but I read the movie version," David said.

"Why do authors write stories about mistaken identity, anyway?" Nathan wanted to know. "I mean, that stuff only happens in fiction. Real people like us can always tell who's who. Right, Nathan?"

"I'm David. *You're* Nathan," David told him.

"Oh yeah, never mind," said Nathan.

"Anyhoo," Martin interrupted. "I'm standing here. I'm waiting. I'm Martin. And you guys seem to be acting really, really, really weird. Tell me why. It's time to spill the beans. Cough up the truth. Let the cat out of the bag. Mollow the pollow . . ."

"That last one's not a real thing," David said.

"Okay, maybe not," Martin admitted. "But I need to know—why are you both stranger than usual, and why are you talking so much about my brother Myron?"

Nathan and David both realized that they *should* tell Martin the truth: that they were talking about Myron because he was living in their house and taking care of them.

But neither boy could bring himself to do so. They stood there silently for what felt like ten minutes.

"Gentlemen, I sense there is a secret among us. And if you remember the speech I gave back on the day I was elected to the Nanny Hall of Fame . . . oh, wait, that wasn't me. Anyway, you both know how I feel about keeping secrets," Martin said.

"No, we don't," Nathan said.

"Not at all," David added.

"Well, I'd like to tell you how I feel about secrets, guys," Martin informed them. "But I can't. I just can't."

More silence from the boys.

"Okay, guys. Here's the deal. I really should go unpack and tell your parents that their favorite person ever is back to bring joy, order, and nummy-nummy-num-num cooking to their lovelier than lovely home. . . ."

Nathan rolled his eyeballs so far that they almost ended up in David's eyes.

Martin continued: "But first, let's talk out all this Myron stuff. You're twins. I'm a twin. And for whatever reason you're curious about my brother Myron. I'll tell you about him. . . ."

More silence from the boys.

"The number one thing you really must know about my long-lost brother Myron Hyron Dyron, my identical twin with whom I shared a mother, a crib, and a pacifier, but not a last name . . . a man whom I haven't seen in over one thousand fortnights . . . is that he is . . . he is . . . he is . . ."

"Standing right here," Myron said from the doorway.

CHAPTER
FIFTEEN

Myron looked at Martin. Martin looked at Myron. Myron looked back. Then Martin did the same.

Somehow, what had just happened was too much for their adult minds to process. Even the fact that combined they technically had the mental brainpower of an almost senior citizen didn't make it any easier to understand.

But Nathan and David knew one thing: effective immediately, they no longer needed the Myron or Martin Evidence Chart. All the evidence in the world was standing right in front of them.

"Is that you, my brother?" Myron shrieked.

"It's *me*," Martin shrieked. "Is that you, my brother?"

"It's *me*," Myron shrieked. "Is that you, my brother?"

"Is that you, my brother?" David shrieked.

"It's *me*," Nathan shrieked. "Is that you, my brother?"

"It's *me*," David shrieked. "Is that you, my brother?"

They all met in the center of the room. Myron hugged David. Martin hugged Nathan. Martin hugged David. Myron hugged Nathan. Nathan and David each hugged a lamp. Then finally, the boys stepped aside so that Myron could hug Martin and Martin could hug Myron.

It was a hug that the men hadn't felt in over fourteen and a half years. And neither man wanted to let go. They squeezed and hugged and blubbered and kept saying each other's names over and over again.

"Oh, Martin!" Myron said.

"Oh, Myron!" Martin said.

"Oh, Martin, Martin!" Myron said.

"Oh, Myron, Myron!" Martin said.

"Oh, Martin, Martin, Martin!" Myron said.

"Oh, Myron, Myron, Myron!" Martin said.

And on it went, until David finally said, "Oh, brother!"

"Yes, it's my brother!" Martin said.

"Yes, it's *my* brother!" Myron said.

"My brother, brother!" Martin said.

"My brother, brother!" Myron said.

"My brother, brother, brother!" Martin said.

"My brother, brother, brother!" Myron said.

Nathan was getting sick from watching them, and he tried to put himself in their place. He wondered if he'd be that happy to see David if they had been apart for nearly fifteen years.

He decided he wouldn't. Not at all.

He also decided that somehow, some way, he'd have to get all this disgusting brotherly hugging to stop.

He ran to the family computer and Googled "how to stop long-lost brothers from hugging" and got . . . nothing. Not a single handy-dandy tip on how to stop twin brothers who hadn't seen each other in a decade and a half to let go of each other and act normal. Well, normal for them, anyway.

He ran upstairs and got the whistle from the one and only time he'd refereed kindergarten basketball (and no, it wasn't *his* fault that Jacob Reiss had ended up stuffed into the home team's basket). He ran back downstairs—where the Martin/Myron hug was still going on—and he was about to blow the whistle when . . .

Mr. and Mrs. Wohlfardt walked into the house.

"Hello, boys; hello, Martin; hello, Myron," said Mrs. Wohlfardt, extremely matter-of-factly.

"Yes, good evening to all four of you," said Mr. Wohlfardt. "Anything interesting happen to anyone today?"

Nathan and David just stared at their parents. As for Myron and Martin, well, they kept right on blubbering and hugging, and didn't even notice that the couple had entered the room.

"We'll just run upstairs and get washed for dinner," said Mrs. Wohlfardt. "I'm sure Martin and Myron will whip up something delicious."

"Indeed," added Mr. Wohlfardt.

With that, they both climbed the stairs.

Considering that Mr. and Mrs. Wohlfardt had often told their boys to pay close attention to things, it was quite shocking that neither parent had seemed to react to suddenly having Martin back in their living room.

"What the heck?" Nathan said to the lamp he'd hugged.

"Yeah, what the heck?" David said to the lamp he'd hugged.

It wasn't surprising that their lamps, like their parents (who were already upstairs), didn't respond.

CHAPTER
SIXTEEN

The thundering footsteps sounded like a sea of cascading bowling balls on the stairs.

"Martin? MARTIN? Are you back, Martin?" Mrs. Wohlfardt screamed as she descended.

"Myron? MYRON? Is that your brother you're hugging, Myron?" Mr. Wohlfardt screamed as he accidentally stepped on the back of Mrs. Wohlfardt's shoe and popped it off while also stomping down the stairs.

Mrs. Wohlfardt shouted, "Ow, my foot!"

so loudly
that it caught
Martin's and Myron's
attention and they
stopped hugging. It
also caught the Taylor
family's attention three houses down and they
stopped eating, but that really wasn't important
at the moment.

Martin smiled, bowed his most regal bow
(which, in fact, he'd learned by watching a
fried chicken restaurant commercial), and
smiled a big smile at Mr. and Mrs. Wohlfardt.

He stepped toward them and kissed Mrs. Wohlfardt's hand, then shook Mr. Wohlfardt's.

"I am, indeed, back," Martin said, speaking in an accent that wasn't quite British, wasn't quite Scottish, and wasn't quite believable. "I have returned from the land of who-knows-where, where who-knows-what happened to who-knows-who. Or to who-knows-*whom*, I should say."

Mr. and Mrs. Wohlfardt seemed to be impressed by that statement, even though clearly it was impossible to follow and meant absolutely nothing.

"We are glad you're here, Martin," Mrs. Wohlfardt said.

Mr. Wohlfardt energetically nodded in agreement, slightly aggravating a crick he'd had in his neck for weeks.

Myron silently listened to all this "welcome back, Martin" chatter. He was smiling at the fact that he and his brother were in the same room for the first time in over 5,400 days. He was certainly glad to see him. But then, suddenly and without warning, two horrifying thoughts popped into his head:

1. *What if Mr. and Mrs. Wohlfardt are so happy that Martin has come back that they instantly rehire him and send me out into the freezing cold?*

2. *What if Mr. and Mrs. Wohlfardt are so happy that Martin has come back that they instantly rehire him and send me out into the freezing cold?*

Myron was so troubled by what he was thinking that he didn't actually stop to realize that thought number 2 was exactly the same as thought number 1. But he decided to take action to prevent the "Martin hired,

Myron fired" plan from happening. He knew the trick would be finding just the right moment to jump in—because everyone was still busy talking about Martin's surprise return.

"I—" Myron said, before getting cut off by Mr. Wohlfardt.

"Boys, you must be delighted to see Martin," Mr. Wohlfardt said. "This reminds me of the time my pet ran away when I was a boy, and oh, was it a happy moment when we were reunited!"

Martin was so giddy at the family's reaction to his return that he didn't even notice that Mr. Wohlfardt had just compared him to a childhood pet.

"I—" Myron said, before again getting cut off by Mr. Wohlfardt.

"Of course, it was my pet snail, Roberto, so he really hadn't gotten far," Mr. Wohlfardt said. "He had only run away about ten feet. And it wasn't really running, I suppose. Might have only been six feet, now that I think of it. Still, I can imagine that you are feeling the same sense of jubilation that I felt when Roberto and I found each other again."

"I—" Myron said, before getting cut off by David.

"It's a good thing, Dad," David said.

"I—" Myron said, before getting cut off by Nathan.

"Yeah, Dad," Nathan agreed. "It's great to see him."

"Now we have twin boys in the house," Mrs. Wohlfardt said, "and twin nannies, too."

Uh-oh, thought Myron. *If Martin heard her, my goose will be on the loose. Or cooked. Or fried. Or whatever that expression is.*

"Um, did I hear that correctly?" Martin wanted to know. "What do you mean by 'twin nannies'?"

Four people then spoke to him—all at the same time.

"You disappeared. Myron appeared. We hired him, Martin," said Mrs. Wohlfardt.

"No nanny, no good behavior, no schoolwork, no good," said Mr. Wohlfardt.

"Myron got here after you left us, Martin, and it's like having you without having you," said Nathan.

"Someday I hope to be the starting catcher for the New York Mets. And, oh yeah, Myron takes care of us now," said David.

"Waaaaaiiiitttt!" Martin yelled, this time without a foreign accent. "Since you all talked at the same time, I didn't understand a word any of you just said."

The two kids and their parents started saying the exact same things at the exact same time once again.

"Hold it! Hold it!" Martin said. "One at a time, puleeze!"

Nathan and David and their mom and dad looked at each other, trying to decide who should speak first. But before any of them could utter a sound, Myron stepped forward and said, quite dramatically:

"I have something to say. Martin, it is delightful to see you. Truly. I have missed you and thought of you often, and looked forward to the day we would once again stand face-to-face, toe-to-toe, and index-finger-to-index-finger. I've greatly enjoyed our monthly one-word e-mails over the years, and seeing you in person is even better. But . . . however . . . alas . . . I have terrible news for you."

"I know," said Martin. "I know."

"You do?" said Myron. "Won't you please tell me, dear brother, whom I have not seen since much before these fine Wohlfardt lads were born?"

"Yes, I do," Martin replied. "It's very clear to me that as the years have passed, you've become very wordy. But we can work on that on my days off, once I unpack and resume my job as the Wohlfardts' nanny."

"Many people have told me I am wordy, long-winded, and the type of person who uses many, many, many words when just a few will do," Myron said. "But that is not the case. I am not wordy, no way, no chance, nohow, not now, and at no time in the past. . . ."

"Zzzzzz," Martin snored.

Myron continued, "At any rate, that is not my terrible news. The news I have is only terrible for *you*, I'm afraid. Because, you see, . . . the job as the Wohlfardts' nanny is filled . . . by me, *moi*, your non-wordy brother . . . Myron Hyron Dyron."

"No! I want my job back!" boomed Martin.

"You can't have it!" boomed Myron. "But there is one thing you *can* have back!"

"What's that?" Martin asked.

"Your hug!" Myron told him. "Because I don't want it anymore! Grrrr . . ."

"Grrrrrrrrrrrr," Martin replied, rolling his *R*s quite dramatically.

CHAPTER
SEVENTEEN

As an airline pilot, Mr. Wohlfardt had quite a bit of experience settling feuds. He was especially proud of the time that twenty-seven passengers had all been booked into the same aisle seat and he calmly settled the matter before any voices were raised. In case you're wondering, eighty-three-year-old Mildred Williams of Kenosha, Wisconsin, ended up in 17C, the prized aisle seat.

He stepped in to try to settle the nanny vs.

nanny debate currently brewing in his living room.

"Myron! Martin! Please!" Mr. Wohlfardt said, standing so close between the men who were arguing that their mustaches tickled his ears. "We must restore peace and order at once! Think of your relationship! Think of how this looks to my boys! Most of all, think of how warmingly delicious a steaming cup of hot cocoa would taste right now."

He wasn't sure why he'd said the last part, but somehow, it was that line that got the men to stop bickering. Mr. Wohlfardt led them, along with his wife, into the kitchen. He directed Nathan and David to go to their rooms to do homework, or clean, or do something productive. They both clomped up the stairs, disappointed at missing the "good stuff," as Nathan called it.

When they got to their door, David yelled,

"Here we go into our room, where we won't be able to hear what you're saying!"

He winked at Nathan and then slammed their bedroom door so that the adults downstairs would *think* that the boys were in their room . . . when, in fact, they were standing silently *outside their bedroom door.*

David put on his Super-Spy Super Hearing Glasses that came in his Super-Sleuth Detective Kit. The glasses didn't actually improve his listening abilities one bit—because they went on his *eyes*. But Nathan stood by hopefully and silently, anxious for updates.

Once in the kitchen, Mr. Wohlfardt began whipping up some steaming hot cocoa as he and his wife addressed the fighting nannies.

"Martin, Myron, what we have here is a dilemma," he told them.

"Indeed we do," his wife continued. "On the one hand, Martin was here for quite a long time, and he gave our boys a fresh start."

"They're having fresh tarts," David whispered to his brother, both assuming that he could hear what Nathan couldn't. Nathan gave him a thumbs-up.

"But on the other hand, Martin," Mr. Wohlfardt said as he plopped the chocolate into the pan, "you quit, went away, and left us, well, nanny-free."

"I believe the correct term is 'nannyless,'" his wife said. "At any rate, all the positive steps our boys had taken quickly disappeared when you did, Martin. Their grades suffered.

Their behavior suffered. Their tidiness suffered . . ."

"And we all suffered," Mr. Wohlfardt added.

"Dad said, 'We're all having supper,' " David whispered to his brother.

Mrs. Wohlfardt went on to explain that when their nannyless lives spiraled out of control, she lost her biggest account at Jordan, Jordan, Jordan, Jordan, and Glerk. With great passion, she even said that if that hadn't happened, by now the name of the business *might* have been changed to Jordan, Jordan, Jordan, Jordan, Glerk, and Wohlfardt. Or perhaps even Jordan, Jordan, Jordan, Jordan, Wohlfardt, and Glerk, because no one especially liked Glerk.

"No one especially likes Glerk," David told his brother.

"I heard that!" Nathan whispered. "Those glasses are so powerful, even *I* can hear better when you're wearing them!"

"Our world was sliding downhill faster than a skier on ice skates covered with banana peels," Mrs. Wohlfardt said.

"They're skiing and having banana peels," David informed his brother.

"And then," Mr. Wohlfardt continued, "just when things seemed darkest, into our lives came Myron."

"It seemed too good to be true," Mrs. Wohlfardt said. "A nanny who looked like you, acted quite a bit like you, and inspired the boys to do better—just as you had, Martin."

"A perfect description of the excellence that is Myron Hyron Dyron, if you ask Myron Hyron Dyron," Myron Hyron Dyron said.

Martin just said, "Harrumph . . ."

Upstairs, Nathan sneezed. David elbowed him.

"Bless you, David," Mrs. Wohlfardt called upstairs.

"It was *me*, Nathan. Thank you, Mom," Nathan said.

"You're welcome, Nathan," Mrs. Wohlfardt said.

"Thank you, Mom," David said.

The debate downstairs raged on. Mr. Wohlfardt, eager to be the voice of reason, poured four cups of hot cocoa, passed them around, and said, "I am sure we can work out this rather sticky situation. Let's look at it this way, shall we?"

Mr. Wohlfardt shook up a can of whipped cream and sprayed a generous amount into Martin's cup.

"That whipped cream represents Martin's job here as our nanny," he said.

"I didn't really want whipped cream," Martin said.

"No, but you *did* want the job," Mr. Wohlfardt told him. "And now you want it again. So please go along with this."

"Very well," Martin said. "You are the boss, boss."

"Thank you. Now remember, this whipped cream represents the job," Mr. Wohlfardt continued as he scooped out the whipped cream from Martin's cup and plopped it into Myron's. "It was Martin's; it's now Myron's."

"So the whipped cream is mine, the job is mine, and that's the end of the story," Myron said, slurping up the whipped cream and getting quite a bit of it on his mustache.

"Big deal," Martin said. "I'll just spray myself another portion."

Martin grabbed the can and sprayed a huge layer of whipped cream onto his cocoa. (He so wanted to spray some into his mouth, but he knew there'd be plenty of time for that later.)

"There," Martin said. "Now I have whipped

cream. And if the whipped cream represents the job, I have that, too."

"No, no, wait, no," Myron sputtered, his arms flailing.

Mr. Wohlfardt hushed Myron and calmly said, "Now, that may seem possible, Martin. But remember, the whipped cream only *represented* the job. As you well know, the fact is, we can't just buy a can of children at the grocery store and spray out two additional boys for you to care for."

"We're getting two more boys," David whispered.

Martin put on his best sad face; it was the one he'd last shown back when he'd lost the kindergarten spelling bee because he couldn't spell *I*.

"So *I'm* out? Gone? Kicked to the curb? Vamoosed?" Martin asked.

"We're getting a moose," David whispered, scrunching up his face and wondering if he could still get a refund on his Super-Spy Super Hearing Glasses.

"Well, not exactly vamoosed, Martin," Mrs. Wohlfardt said. "Because, you see, it's time to start a new chapter."

CHAPTER
EIGHTEEN

Mrs. Wohlfardt could see that her husband's use of whipped cream may have been delicious, but it certainly wasn't leading toward a happy resolution of the two-nanny problem. She could also envision everything going wildly out of control, with Myron and Martin ending up in a frenzied whipped cream–squirting battle. The thought made her want to laugh, of course, but she knew this was no laughing matter.

So she gave her husband a look that said *Let me try*, and she proceeded to make a speech similar to one she had recently made when she found two office workers photocopying their bare feet at Jordan, Jordan, Jordan, Jordan, and Glerk.

Upstairs, the boys slithered, snakelike, to the top of the stairs, remaining just out of sight, for a better chance of hearing the conversation. It wasn't a good thing for them to do, because private adult conversations are supposed to remain private adult conversations. But frankly, Nathan and David wanted to know more about the moose they were getting.

Mrs. Wohlfardt started her remarks in a very businesslike manner. "Men," Mrs. Wohlfardt said, "we all want what is best for the company, er, the boys, don't we?"

Myron and Martin nodded. Mr. Wohlfardt did too.

Mrs. Wohlfardt continued, "Nathan and David come first. But also, we want what's best for you, Martin, and you, Myron. You deserve consideration. You deserve to treat each other with love and respect. And most of all, after being apart for so long, you deserve to be together."

Myron and Martin nodded. Mr. Wohlfardt did too.

"Sending one of you away would, of course, make our boys sad. It would also put an end to your newfound brotherlinessness," Mrs. Wohlfardt added, wondering if perhaps she'd said one "ness" too many.

Myron and Martin nodded. Mr. Wohlfardt did too.

"And so, I suggest that you *both* stay for thirty days," she continued. "You jointly take care of Nathan and David, working side by side as total equals. You take time to enjoy each other's company. And within those thirty days, I'm quite sure we'll find an answer that will satisfy everyone. Good, Myron? Good, Martin?"

Myron and Martin pondered the idea.

Mr. Wohlfardt shook his head.

"Dear," he whispered to his wife, "having two nannies also means we'd be paying two S-A-L-A-R-I-E-S."

Mrs. Wohlfardt whispered back, "Yes, but only for thirty days, dear . . ."

"Even so," Mr. Wohlfardt mouthed to his wife.

Noticing Mr. Wohlfardt's concern, Myron and Martin quickly worked together to figure out what S-A-L-A-R-I-E-S spelled. Once they got it, they immediately huddled and whispered back and forth to each other. In a matter of seconds, with hands cupped over their mustaches, they discussed the fact that if Martin had gotten the job back, Myron would've been out of work, and out of a salary. Similarly, if the Wohlfardts had decided that Myron would stay, Martin would be unemployed and unpaid. So they quickly decided that spending thirty days together was a smart way for each man to show that *he* should be their one and only nanny.

"We accept," both men said to Mr. and Mrs. Wohlfardt.

"This means the problem is solved," Mrs. Wohlfardt said.

"This means we once again have peace and harmony in the house," Mr. Wohlfardt said. He and his wife then went upstairs to share the news with the boys (who had already heard and were busy slithering back to their rooms at record speed).

"This means *war*!" Myron and Martin both declared under their breath, and stared menacingly into each other's eyes. Then they had a frenzied whipped cream–squirting battle, just as Mrs. Wohlfardt had feared they might.

In thirty days, one would stay and one would go. *If* the nannies . . . and the family . . . and the house . . . made it that far.

CHAPTER
NINETEEN

Yes, Myron and Martin were engaged in a battle. But they were, first and foremost, brothers. So that night, Myron invited Martin to share his room.

"I will be happy to bunk with you," Martin said. "But first, you must admit that you are not sharing your room with me. Rather, you must agree that it's *my* room and *I* am sharing it with *you*."

Myron rolled his eyes and said, "Fine, sleep on the couch in the living room."

"I'll do just that," said Martin. "I will sleep on the couch in the living room, because that is what I choose to do. It is a wonderful couch, and I will sleep on the couch in the living room. I will sleep on the couch in the living room. Please don't make me sleep on the couch in the living room."

Myron smiled and invited his brother into the bedroom.

A grateful Martin looked at the room and said hello to all the furniture that used to be his (calling each piece by name, which was weird). Then he flipped open the sofa bed—or as he called it, Sofia Couchowitz.

Myron knew what Martin would say next.

"So plush. So comfy. So . . . enjoy sleeping here," Martin told him.

"Not. A. Chance." Myron laughed, plopping onto his own bed.

"I wouldn't treat my twin brother like this," Martin said.

"What would you do?" Myron wanted to know.

"If there was one full-size, deluxe bed and one sleeper sofa, I would give my brother the bed and I'd take the sleeper sofa," Martin said.

"So? That's what you got!" Myron told him. "We're good. And speaking of good, good night."

Myron's head hit the pillow and he was asleep in a matter of seconds. As for Martin, he creaked his body into the creaky sofa bed, and began making a list of the ways he was going to win back his job, his full salary, his bed, and his reputation as the world's greatest nanny.

Many of the items on the list were things he'd never tried before. Things like hard work. Dedication. Creativity. And thoughtfulness.

"Yes, I will give the Wohlfardts everything I have," he announced to no one as he started falling asleep. "I will outdo my brother at everything. And in thirty days"—yawn—"the kingdom shall be"—yawn—"mine! Mine, mine, mine, mine, mine!"

"Mine," his brother mindlessly gurgled in his sleep.

The next morning, Myron and Martin awoke at precisely the same moment: twenty-one seconds past 6:14 a.m. Each immediately turned his sleep clothes inside out and counted that as getting dressed, then raced to the kitchen to make an impressive breakfast for Nathan and David.

The boys, meanwhile, showed up at the breakfast table extra early; they both understood that this was the first day of Operation: Make Myron and Martin Do Anything and Everything We Ask.

From the second the boys slid into their seats, it was very clear there was a major competition going on between the nannies.

"Good morning, men. Welcome to the best restaurant in town, Chez Martin!"

"What's for breakfast?" Nathan asked.

"Hold on, Neptune!" Myron said, still apparently not willing or able to call the boys by their actual names. "Don't settle for anything less than the world-famous fine cuisine at Myron's Place!"

"Get ready to enjoy some cranberry pancakes à la Martin!" Martin proclaimed.

"But first . . . have a delicious helping or twelve of delectable pie à la Myron!" Myron said.

"What, no fresh-squeezed orange-carrot-mango juice?" David cried.

"And where's our farm-fresh milk?" Nathan asked.

Martin ran out of the room, and a moment later, the boys swore they heard a cow in the den. Martin returned with two glasses of smooth, creamy, insanely fresh milk.

"Paper napkins?" David scoffed.

"No, cloth napkins!" Martin offered, exchanging the paper goods for two fine linen napkins.

"Wait . . . hand-knitted napkins!" Myron countered.

"Plastic forks?" Nathan sneered.

"Certainly not! Sterling silver!" Martin said, swooping in and switching the utensils.

"Put those down; I've got solid-gold forks!" Myron said. And he did.

"We're supposed to slice our own food?" David wondered.

"No! I'll pre-slice the entire meal for you!" Martin declared.

"I'll pre-*chew* it!" Myron replied.

"What's with you guys?" David asked the nannies (though he totally knew what was going on).

"Nothing," Martin said. "We just want to treat you the best we can."

"Exactly," Myron said. "The very best we can."

The boys smiled. They knew for sure that *they* would be the winners of the Martin-Myron challenge; they'd be treated like royalty as the nannies tried to outdo each other all month long.

"This is gonna be good," David whispered to his brother. "So good."

"Yeah," Nathan whispered back.

He then addressed the nannies: "Oh, Myron, Martin, please wipe our mouths and then carry us to school on your backs."

CHAPTER
TWENTY

After Nathan and David had gone to school (and no, Myron and Martin *didn't* carry them), Myron and Martin sat down for a talk. They realized that they were in for a month of getting bossed around by the boys, and they didn't like it. Not one bit.

"Our having to compete means that they can ask us for anything, and if we don't do it, we could lose the job," Myron said.

"Quite true, my bro, quite true," Martin replied.

"So right here, right now, we should agree that *we* are in charge," Myron said, pointing his thumb at himself and his pinky at Martin for emphasis. "They can ask for the moon, but we don't have to give it to them!"

Martin said he agreed with Myron (though in the back of his mind, he was thinking about how he'd go about getting the moon for the boys).

"We simply cannot go overboard to win them over. Let's take the sacred family pledge to seal the deal," Myron said.

"Yes, let's," Martin said, still wondering about the best way to actually deliver the moon to Nathan and David.

Both men spoke: "To honor my brother, and my family, I will do good stuff and not do wrong stuff and stuff like that."

Then they high-fived, and that was that.

Or was it?

Because even though they'd vowed not to

go to extreme measures to please the boys, later that afternoon, that's exactly what each nanny did.

When Nathan and David walked into the house after school, each boy threw a huge stack of raffle tickets onto the kitchen counter.

"What are those?" Myron wanted to know.

"Yes, what are those?" Martin echoed.

"Raffle tickets," David said.

"Oh," Myron said. Then he went back to

what he'd been doing—autographing all the melons in the kitchen.

Why was he autographing all the melons in the kitchen? Because, you see, Martin had already signed all the lemons—which, by the way, is spelled with the exact same letters as "melons," though Martin didn't know that.

"We have to sell them to raise money for a new piano that's needed in the school's music room," Nathan told him. "Every kid is responsible for selling fifty tickets."

"Yeah," David continued. "And the prize is the school's old piano, plus free music lessons for a year from Mrs. Garvett, the music teacher."

"Sounds like a worthy project," Martin said. "And we certainly wish you luck with it. Don't we, Myron?"

"Indeed we do, Martin," Myron answered. "Good luck indeed, indeed."

"That's it? Just good luck?" Nathan asked.

"What else is there?" Martin said. "It's *your* project, after all."

"Not ours," Myron added.

In an effort to totally take advantage of the nannies' need to impress, Nathan and David then strongly suggested that Myron and Martin help them sell their tickets. Martin and Myron looked at each other and nodded in a way that said that merely helping would be acceptable.

"C'mon, guys, we can walk around the neighborhood with you," Myron offered.

"Together?" Nathan said. "That's no good. You can't have two ticket sellers knocking on doors. People will get confused. No one will buy from either one of us."

"The baboon is right," David said. "We can't do this together."

"Okay, Dave, you come with me," Martin

said, despite his agreement to not get involved. "We'll cover the houses from Flerch Street down to Shumway Avenue. Nathan, you and Myron go up Flerch to Adams Lane."

Myron said that sounded good, and that they should all meet back at the house in an hour.

Nathan grabbed his tickets, and he and Myron left through the front door.

David grabbed his pack of tickets and popped out the back door, with Martin running slightly behind.

"Okay, kid, gimme the tickets," Martin said.

"Huh? I can carry them," David told him.

"Yeah, great, but I wanna buy them," Martin explained.

"How many?" David asked.

"All of them," Martin said, whipping out a fifty-dollar bill and putting it into the boy's hand.

"You don't have to do that, Martin," David said, though he certainly was thrilled to have sold the whole pack of tickets in less than forty-seven seconds.

"My pleasure, kid. It's what special people do for people they care about. And I'm a special people. Um, person. Just remember that—Martin cares about you and wants the best for you, and if giving you the best means buying fifty tickets to win a broken-down piano, that's what I'll do!"

It's probably no surprise that just down the street, Myron did pretty much the exact same thing for Nathan. And after showing Nathan the fifty-dollar bill, Myron left him standing on the street as he ran into a bank and got change for the fifty . . . so it wouldn't appear as if one person had bought all the tickets.

"There you go," said Myron as he handed Nathan the money. "One twenty, one ten, two fives, three one-dollar bills, two quarters, eleven dimes, seven nickels and five pennies."

"Thanks so much, Myron," Nathan said. "But that's only forty-five bucks; you're five dollars short."

Myron said he was just trying to check Nathan's math skills, but Nathan was pretty sure Myron was just trying to hold on to his five dollars.

At the same time, Martin ran into a different bank and got change for David as well. He handed the boy a ton of small bills and coins, which David quickly realized totaled thirty-five dollars.

Martin said he was just trying to check David's math skills, but David was pretty sure Martin was just trying to hold on to his fifteen dollars.

Either way, with all their tickets sold, Martin and David sat on a park bench and waited for the hour to pass.

Myron and Nathan did the same—different park, different bench, but identical time-wasting idea.

So much for Myron and Martin not going overboard for the boys.

So much for the sacred pledge.

This was *war*.

CHAPTER
TWENTY-ONE

It didn't end with the nannies buying all the raffle tickets. As the days and weeks passed, Myron and Martin continually tried to outshine each other to impress the Wohlfardt family. The men were constantly exhausted as they went out of their way to show how they could be nannies, super-nannies, super-duper nannies, and super-super-duper nannies.

When David said, "It would be nice if you'd do my laundry," that's what Myron did. He also did Nathan's. Then Martin washed, dried, and ironed it all again.

When Nathan suggested that his bicycle could sure use a paint job, that's what Martin did.

When David didn't feel like delivering the newspapers on his afternoon paper route, that's what Myron and Martin did.

When Nathan didn't have time to make his mother a birthday card, that's what Myron did (he wrote, DEAR MOMMMMY, and Martin then changed it to what he knew was correct: DEER MOMY).

When Nathan and David asked for before-bed hot fudge sundaes delivered to their room, they each got one every night at 8:18 p.m.

The more attention and special treatment the boys got, the more they requested. Martin and Myron were competing themselves into a constant state of tiredness.

And what's worse is that after spending fifty dollars each on raffle tickets, neither nanny won the old piano and music lessons. (Incredibly, Mrs. Mildred Williams—the woman from Kenosha, Wisconsin, who'd ended up in seat 17C on Mr. Wohlfardt's plane—had recently moved to Screamersville and won the piano and lessons. She was one lucky person!)

Of course, with about a week to go in the nanny competition, the month hadn't been *all* bad. Martin and Myron did enjoy spending time with each other. They played games from their childhood, including Chabble (their specially created combination of chess and Scrabble, using a Scrabble board, all the vowel tiles, and chess pieces). They took long runs in opposite directions together, talked about friends and teachers from their hometown, and generally clowned around in ways they hadn't done since, well, ever.

But there was still the matter of what to do about how Nathan and David were taking advantage of them, and about the competition that would be ending soon.

As it turns out, they didn't have to do anything about those things. Because one evening during that final week, Mr. and Mrs. Wohlfardt called an urgent family meeting, and summoned both boys and both nannies to the den—at once.

The Wohlfardts had never had an urgent family meeting before. Sure, they'd had chats. And talks. And a few "idea exchange sessions," as Mr. Wohlfardt had called them. But the words "family meeting" scared Nathan. And David. And Myron. And Martin. Hearing the word "urgent" before "family meeting" was absolutely petrifying to them.

Martin stared at Mr. and Mrs. Wohlfardt, expecting to hear one of them say, "You're fired." Myron stared as well, expecting to hear the same thing. And judging by the stern looks on their parents' faces, even Nathan and David were wondering if *they'd* be fired.

Can parents fire their kids? Nah, Nathan thought. He did, however, remind himself to Google the subject later.

Mrs. Wohlfardt spoke first. "As you well remember, it was *my* idea to ask Myron and Martin to stay for thirty days. . . ."

"Yes, Mother," Nathan said.

"Yes, Mother," David said.

"Yes, Mother," Martin said.

"Yes, Mother," Myron said.

Mrs. Wohlfardt continued, "But that turned out to be a terrible idea."

"Terrible," Mr. Wohlfardt echoed.

"Myron and Martin, we expected that you would show us your best selves during your time here together. And you have," Mrs. Wohlfardt told them. "But . . ."

"But?" Nathan asked.

"But?" David asked.

"But?" Martin asked.

"But?" Myron asked.

"But as you've worked your hardest to prove how wonderful you are," Mr. Wohlfardt said, "we've seen quite a competition taking place. And we know that a certain two little monsters have made your lives miserable, taking advantage of your good nature."

Nathan gulped.

David gulped.

"Oh, I don't mind," Myron said.

"Me either," Martin said.

"Yes, you do, Myron," Mr. Wohlfardt told him. "You cried to me about it this morning."

"You cried?" Martin asked. "Ha ha ha ha ha!"

"You blubbered to me too, Martin, just a few minutes after your brother did," Mr. Wohlfardt said to Martin. "And yet now you say you don't mind how the boys have treated you. Apparently brothers who cry together also lie about things together."

"Technically, we weren't together when we cried," Martin feebly pointed out.

"Who cried *better*?" Myron wanted to know, looking for any possible advantage over his brother.

Mr. Wohlfardt went on to tell the men that it *wasn't* okay that Nathan and David had made the nannies do their chores, their school projects, and everything else that the boys were usually responsible for.

"For one thing," he said, "you are here to help the boys do their very best. All they've done the past few weeks is prove how sloppy, lazy, and inconsiderate they can be by having you do everything for them."

"Plus," Mrs. Wohlfardt continued, "I'd very much like to know which one of you men wrote David's school report on JFK. . . ."

"That was me," Myron said meekly.

"Well, it was nicely done, Myron," Mrs. Wohlfardt told him. "But you wrote five hundred words about the thirty-fifth president of the United States."

"Yes, I did," Myron said.

"Myron? How could you?" David blurted out. "The assignment was to write a report about JFK the New York airport—not the president!"

"Is it *his* fault that you asked him to write the paper and then handed it in without reading it?" Mr. Wohlfardt wanted to know.

"No, Dad," David said.

"I'm surprised at you!" Martin whispered to Myron.

"I'm surprised at you!" Nathan whispered to David.

"And, Martin," Mrs. Wohlfardt said, "I've seen you tiptoeing next door to feed the Kendall family's cat while they're away, haven't I?"

"Yes, Mrs. Wohlfardt. I just love that itty-bitty kitty," Martin said in a sickeningly cute voice.

"Very nice, Martin," she responded. "But they hired *Nathan* for that job, didn't they?"

"Well, yes, but I *do* love that itty-bitty kitty," Martin told her.

"Nathan, since the Kendall family went away, how many times would you say you've fed the cat?" Mrs. Wohlfardt inquired.

"Not even once," Nathan admitted. "Martin's done it every time."

"I'm surprised at you!" Myron whispered to Martin.

"I'm surprised at you!" David whispered to Nathan.

"It's just so itty-bitty," Martin said.

Mr. and Mrs. Wohlfardt then listed several other instances where the boys had made the nannies do their work. It was not a happy meeting.

"In conclusion," Mr. Wohlfardt said in the sternest tone he could manage without straining his voice, "there is one week to go in this double-nanny experiment. One week to change your behavior, boys, and return to being the responsible students and fine, upstanding citizens that you know you can be. And one week for you, Myron and Martin, to show that you're here for the good of our boys, not just to win a job."

The boys and the nannies all apologized, and all said they would do better from then on.

And it seemed as if they all meant it. As they ran upstairs, Nathan and David didn't expect hot fudge sundaes to be delivered to their room. Neither nanny offered to wash, dry, fold, and iron the boys' laundry. And Martin didn't think about ways he could give the kids the moon (as he'd still been doing for weeks).

Sometimes an urgent family meeting can make quite a difference.

CHAPTER
TWENTY-TWO

Quite a difference indeed.

Through the week that followed the urgent family meeting, Martin and Myron were the *perfect* nannies. They helped Nathan and David, but not too much. They guided them in their chores, but didn't actually do them for the boys. They assisted them with school matters, but it was encouragement, not actual work.

For Nathan and David, it was the end of

the good days. But somewhere, deep down, they knew that taking responsibility for their own efforts was the right thing to do. In a funny way, it felt good.

Nathan began feeding the Kendall family's cat all by himself, and he, too, fell deeply in love with the itty-bitty kitty. He also took it upon himself to clean up the giant-wiant mess that the itty-bitty kitty had made around her food bowl. For the first time in a long time, Nathan was taking care of business, and it made him proud of himself. What's more, being proud of himself made him proud of himself.

As for David, he started doing things for

himself again too. And like his brother, he thought it felt good to be taking action rather than taking a nap while relying on others to take action for him. It's true that his shirts weren't as neatly folded as when the nannies folded them, or that his bed wasn't made with the same careful four-hour dedication Myron had provided, but that was okay with David. And he was certainly glad that he'd never again have to have his teacher hand back a report with "JFK the airport, not the president!!!!" written in big red letters across the top.

For the nannies, it was an easygoing,

joyful week. Truthfully, it was so much fun working as a team to help the boys, both nannies pretty much forgot about the quickly approaching day when the Wohlfardts would decide which one could stay, and which one had to leave.

Mr. and Mrs. Wohlfardt were thrilled at how smoothly the week went; they loved seeing great nanny cooperation for the benefit of Nathan and David. But . . .

They were extremely fretful about the decision that had to be made on the evening of the thirtieth day of the Martin vs. Myron challenge.

What's more, there were quite a few decisions to be made about *how* the final decision would actually be made.

For one thing, the Wohlfardt parents wondered if they should be the ones to make the Martin or Myron decision. Should they ask the boys for their opinions? And if they did that, what if Nathan ended up wanting one nanny and David chose the other?

Was it better for Nathan and David to be *told* which nanny was staying?

At times, Mrs. Wohlfardt wondered if *both* nannies could somehow stay. Maybe Myron could take care of David, and Martin could take care of Nathan. Or vice versa. No, she figured, because that would mean two full-time S-A-L-A-R-I-E-S.

At times, Mr. Wohlfardt wondered if they needed *either* nanny.

The big decision was pretty much the only thing the Wohlfardt parents talked about. They asked friends, relatives, and coworkers what they thought they should do. But no one provided any real help.

Meanwhile, Nathan and David were on their best behavior all week. But they too were worried about which nanny would be holding on to his job.

"I think Mom's gonna want Martin," Nathan said.

"Nope," David said. "Mom's more on Myron's side, and I think Dad likes Martin better."

Nathan disagreed. "Dad's totally in favor of Myron staying," he said. "I've seen them watching football together."

"Myron doesn't *care* about football, and he doesn't *know anything* about football," David told him. "I heard him tell Dad he used to play quarterback, halfback, and dollarback. There's no such thing as a dollarback, except when you're getting change in a store."

"Even so," Nathan said. "Mom'll vote for Martin, and Dad'll vote for Myron."

David thought about that for a minute.

Then he asked his brother which nanny *he'd* vote for.

Nathan told his brother he wished he hadn't asked. Because on the one hand, he explained, Martin was the first nanny to really help the boys become better brothers, better kids, better students, better everythings. So they should always be grateful for that. But on the other hand, Martin left them, which wasn't nice. But on the third hand, when he left, they fell back into their rotten habits, which made it seem that they really did need Martin. But on the fourth hand, when Myron took over, *he* helped them find their way back to being good kids. He was a nice guy, and he kind of did most of the stuff that Martin had done for them.

David said he pretty much agreed. He said that if Martin hadn't left, they'd never have known Myron, and they'd have been just fine. But also, if Martin hadn't come back, they would have been fine with Myron.

And back and forth and back and forth they went. There really was no easy answer.

CHAPTER
TWENTY-THREE

On the night before the thirtieth day, no one in the Wohlfardt household slept well at all.

Mrs. Wohlfardt tossed and turned, dreaming that she was in a car and had reached a fork in the road. One direction would take her to the town of Martinville. But if she chose the other route, she'd end up in Myron Falls.

Mr. Wohlfardt tossed and turned, dreaming that he was on a game show, and the final, million-dollar question was "Who is the right nanny for your family?" The clock was ticking, and he needed to come up with an answer. Fortunately, the game show host kept pausing for commercials—including one for the airline that employed Mr. Wohlfardt as a pilot. Even better, Mr. Wohlfardt was the star of the commercial in his dreams, tap dancing while singing the jingle "If You Don't Fly Us, You Should Try Us!"

David tossed and turned, dreaming that Myron and Martin were jumping on his bed, soaring higher and higher toward the ceiling. The funny thing was, while he was dreaming that, the nannies actually *were* jumping on his bed. But that's another story.

Nathan tossed and turned, dreaming that Uncle Pipperman was all out of pencil and rice salad, and had lost the recipe when he accidentally baked it into his famous chocolate-chip chicken lemon fritters.

Back in their room, Myron tossed and turned so much that he rolled all the way onto Martin's sleeper couch. Fortunately, Martin had tossed and turned in the exact opposite direction, and he rolled over his brother and ended up on Myron's full-size bed.

When morning came, the four Wohlfardts and the two nannies were sleepy, groggy, and foggy. None of them were in the mood to face the big decision.

At breakfast, Nathan almost fell asleep in his cereal bowl. David almost fell asleep in his scrambled eggs. Mr. Wohlfardt put pancake syrup in his coffee, and Mrs. Wohlfardt dipped her tea bag in her orange juice.

Myron and Martin each did their very best to stay awake while serving breakfast and doing the dishes. Then they each excused themselves and went off to different, faraway areas of the house.

That was fine with the Wohlfardts, of course; since it was a Sunday morning, none of them had anywhere they needed to be. As soon as breakfast was over, they each crawled back into their beds to try to get a little extra rest.

In the basement sat Myron, silently thinking about the situation at hand. He took out a fancy notepad and scrawled down his thoughts.

In the attic sat Martin, listening to a tuba concerto while thinking about the situation at hand. He took out a roll of calculator paper he had found on Mrs. Wohlfardt's home office desk and scrawled down his thoughts.

Several hours later, Mr. Wohlfardt woke up to find a note pinned to his pajamas.

He quickly woke up his wife, who found a similar note pinned to *her* pajamas.

"This can't be good," Mrs. Wohlfardt said with a sigh.

Mr. Wohlfardt grabbed his eyeglasses, unpinned his note, and read it aloud:

Dear Mr. Wohlfardt (and Mrs. Wohlfardt, too, of course),

This is a note from me, Myron. You know, Myron Hyron Dyron. I suppose you're wondering why you woke up to find a note pinned to you, Mr. Wohlfardt. Well, I wanted to make sure you saw it immediately after your nap.

This note hasn't been easy to write, Mr. Wohlfardt. For one thing, this pen isn't very good—there's some

kind of fuzz on the tip, and the
ink comes out kind of scratchy. For
another thing, it's never easy
to express just what's in your brain,
and that is something I very much
want to do right now.

"Martin was right," Mr. Wohlfardt told his
wife. "Myron *is* pretty wordy."
He continued reading:

What's in my brain, Mr. Wohlfardt,
is a deep respect for each member
of your family. Your boys are
delightful, and you and your wife
have treated me with kindness and
friendship. More than just two
bosses, you've been like a fifth mother
(Mrs. Wohlfardt) and seventeenth father
(you) to me.

I would stay here forever, forever, forever, forever if I could. But I realize that if I stay, you will most certainly decide that I've won the job, which means that my remarkable twin brother, Martin, would be out of work. He'd have nowhere to live. No income. And nowhere to live. Sorry, I already said that part.

I do love your family, but I love my own just a teensy-weensy bit more, so I am going to step aside so that Martin can stay. He is, after all, my twin brother, which I think you already know.

Please tell Nazuki I say good-bye. And please ask Nazuki to tell Dazuki I say good-bye. Although I suppose you could tell that to Dazuki. It doesn't really matter to me who tells him, as long as Dazuki knows I say good-bye.

Also, please remind the boys to do their homework every night, to keep their rooms clean, and to brush their teeth twice a day. (Also, please tell Nazuki that the smaller one is the toothbrush and the bigger one is the hairbrush. He sometimes mixes those up.)

So long, Mr. Wohlfardt, and happy flying!

"Oh dear, Myron is leaving us because he wants the best for his brother," Mrs. Wohlfardt said. "That is so very sweet and considerate."

"I suppose it is," Mr. Wohlfardt agreed. "And it certainly takes us off the hook in terms of having to decide which nanny stays and which one goes. Martin gets the job."

Interestingly, neither Wohlfardt parent questioned the names Nazuki and Dazuki. But realizing their stressful time was over, Mr. and Mrs. Wohlfardt each took a deep breath for the first time all week.

CHAPTER
TWENTY-FOUR

Unfortunately, their sense of relief lasted about as long as their deep breaths did.

Why? Because of the long note that was still pinned to Mrs. Wohlfardt. She unpinned and unrolled the note, borrowed her husband's eyeglasses, and proceeded to read:

Hello, Mrs. Wohlfardt,

It's Martin here at the other side of the pencil. By the way, did you know that the pencil was invented in the 1500s? It was. But listen, I came back to my job because I wanted to do my job. And it's a job that is a job that I enjoy doing. But you had already hired someone else for my job. Okay, I'll stop saying the word "job."

Anyhoo, over the past month, you've given me a chance to prove that I should be your nanny. You've also given me the chance to get to know my brother Myron Hyron Dyron better than I ever thought I could. And do you know what? I think he's exactly like me, which means he's a pretty amazing guy.

I am quite sure that when

you tell us which nanny you've picked as the winner of the competition, it will be me. But I can't be here when you make that announcement. Because, you see, I can't let you hurt my brother's feelings that way.

And so, it is with a heavy heart and an even heavier suitcase that I say farewell once again. I really hate to be saying good-bye this way, but I can't stand the thought of looking into the eyes of Nathan and David and telling them I'm leaving for a second time.

I hope you understand.

I hope they understand.

Because really, I don't understand.

I wish I could stay. And please treat my brother well.

Love,

Martin

"Nooooooooooooooooooooooooooooooo oooooooooooooo!" Mrs. Wohlfardt moaned. "Martin is leaving too!"

Mr. Wohlfardt couldn't believe it.

"He's going for the same reason—so his brother gets the job instead," he said.

"They are being so kind to each other," Mrs. Wohlfardt said. "But in doing so, they're being *rotten* to us."

CHAPTER
TWENTY-FIVE

As Mr. and Mrs. Wohlfardt got dressed, they did what they both knew was the only logical thing to do.

They panicked.

They were used to losing nannies. It had happened many, many times before. And they were even used to reading an "I'm leaving" letter from Martin—that had happened before too.

But *this* time, they were losing not one but

two nannies at the same moment. They didn't have any experience with that. In fact, they were pretty sure no family had ever lost two nannies that way.

They could hardly blame Myron and Martin, of course. By quitting, each brother was being selfless and caring, and deep down, the boys' parents admired them for that.

But now the Wohlfardts would be nanny-less again. And somehow, as Mr. Wohlfardt pointed out, they had to break the doubly sad bulletin to Nazuki and Dazuki. Er, Nathan and David.

Before sharing the bad, bad news with the boys, Mrs. Wohlfardt pressed speed dial number 1 on her phone to make the call she'd made so many times before—to the nanny employment agency to start the search for another new caretaker.

After she hung up, Mr. and Mrs. Wohlfardt

left their bedroom and knocked on the boys' door.

"Come in," Nathan said sleepily.

David woke up as his parents entered the room. Both boys sat up in their beds.

"What's wrong, Mom and Dad?" Nathan asked. He'd seen *that look* on their faces before.

"It's day thirty. Did you make a decision about who's staying and who's going?" David asked. "Because if you can't decide, we'd be happy to decide for you."

"Yes," Nathan said. "At the count of three, we'll tell you who we want. One . . . two . . . three . . ."

"M—" David started.

"M—" Nathan started.

But their dad interrupted before they could say either "yron" or "artin."

"Guys, guys, it doesn't matter who you

want," their dad said. "Because I'm afraid we've got some news you're not going to like."

"Boys," their mother said as tenderly as possible, "they're both . . . gone."

Nathan and David didn't understand what their mother meant. So she and Mr. Wohlfardt explained the whole thing about the notes, and about each nanny leaving so his brother could stay and have the job.

Nathan cried a little. So did David. But neither boy really knew if he was crying because Myron and Martin were gone or because the nannies were being so kind to each other.

In a way, it wasn't important. Because crying is crying, and gone is gone. And as the family would see when they went downstairs to check the nannies' now empty, formerly shared bedroom, Myron Hyron Dyron and Martin Healey Discount were gone for sure.

CHAPTER
TWENTY-SIX

It used to be that when Mrs. Wohlfardt called the employment agency, it took them a while to round up some possible nanny candidates for the boys. That's because word had spread around town that Nathan and David were impossible to deal with, and no one wanted to take (or even interview for) the job.

But recently, the boys' troublesome reputation had begun to fade away.

So it was only slightly surprising that just an hour after Mrs. Wohlfardt made the call, the front doorbell rang.

"That couldn't be a new nanny just yet," Mrs. Wohlfardt said as she ran to answer the door.

But it was.

A new nanny.

At the Wohlfardt front door.

This nanny didn't have a bushy mustache. In fact, as the boys saw when they rushed to the door, this person had no facial hair at all. Because it was a different type of person than they'd gotten used to lately. It was, in fact . . .

A woman.

A female.

A she.

As Mrs. Wohlfardt welcomed her into their home, the nanny said, "Hello, my name is Mary. I'm here for the nanny position."

Mr. and Mrs. Wohlfardt introduced the boys to Mary, then asked them to leave the room so they could discuss the job with her.

The boys stomped into the kitchen to make a sandwich and, naturally, a mess.

A few minutes later, Mr. and Mrs. Wohlfardt concluded the interview by hiring Mary to be the boys' newest nanny. Then they called the twins back into the room. Once Nathan and David had plopped onto the floor, Mrs. Wohlfardt asked the boys to tell Mary all about themselves: where they went to school, what they liked to do, their favorite foods, and so on.

Nathan and David told her plenty. And somehow, strangely, the boys got the feeling that Mary already knew everything they told her.

This is pretty creepy, David thought.

It sure is, Nathan thought, even though David hadn't said *This is pretty creepy* out loud—which was, in fact, even creepier.

Mary seemed nice enough, and she told the boys that she used to be a superstar college basketball player, which they both thought was totally cool.

Then Mary asked, "Do you have any questions for me?"

David blurted out, "What's your full name?

"Mary Huron Delp," she said.

"Another MHD," David whispered to his brother.

"I was thinking the same thing," Nathan whispered back.

"What were you saying?" Mary asked.

"Oh, nothing," Nathan told her. "It's just funny, because you have the exact same initials

as our last two nannies, Myron Hyron Dyron and Martin Healey Discount."

"Quite a coincidence." Mr. Wohlfardt laughed.

"Indeed." Mrs. Wohlfardt laughed.

"*I'll* say!" David said.

"Me too!" Nathan added.

"It's not really a coincidence at all," Mary told them. "Because, you see, Myron and Martin are my twin brothers."

Mr. and Mrs. Wohlfardt both fell off the couch. And David and Nathan fell off the floor—which, as you might imagine, wasn't easy.

That was about as shocked as the four Wohlfardts had ever been. They were all speechless as they thought about the fact that Mary and Martin and Myron were sister and brother and brother.

No one said anything at all for quite a long time. In fact, it was Mary who finally broke the silence. Sitting opposite the four Wohlfardts, Mary cheerily said . . .

"Yes, Myron and Martin are my brothers. And say, here they come now!"

CHAPTER
TWENTY-SEVEN

Yes, Myron Hyron Dyron was back. And Martin Healey Discount was back. In they walked, arm in arm, waving and smiling and creating quite a stir.

"Hello-de-lo-ho-de-lo-lo!" they sang together, having rehearsed that phrase since age three, but never having had a chance to use it in public before.

"Martin!" Nathan screamed.

"Nathan!" Martin screamed.

"Myron!" David screamed.

"Droogy!" Myron screamed.

"Brother!" Mary screamed.

"Sister!" Myron and Martin screamed.

"You're back?" Mr. Wohlfardt exclaimed.

"But we thought . . . ," Mrs. Wohlfardt said.

"You thought that I was leaving because I wanted Myron to have the job," Martin said. "And I truly did."

"And you thought *I* was leaving because I wanted Martin to have the job," Myron said. "And I truly did."

"But we ran into each other at the bus station, where I was about to board a bus heading north-southwest, and I saw that Myron was planning to travel south-northeast," Martin said. "And we realized we'd both quit as your nanny for the exact same reason—and that in doing so, we left you without anyone to watch the boys."

"Poor Nub and Dub," Myron whined. "We didn't mean to do that at all. Really, we didn't. Really. Really. You have to believe us. Really."

"Stop it, Myron," Martin said. "But he's telling the truth. And that, my friends, is why we've come back to the home of the loving Wohlfardtos!"

"Please don't ever call us that again," Mr. Wohlfardt said, scowling.

"I won't," Martin told him apologetically.

"Don't worry about the boys," Mary told her

brothers. "Because I can assure you they will be well taken care of from now on."

"Indeed they will," said Myron. "Because we have a well-thought-out plan. Listen to this . . ."

"I want to tell them," Martin said.

"No, I do," Myron insisted.

"Me," Martin said.

"Me," Myron said.

"It was half my idea," Martin said.

"Then tell them your half," Myron replied. "And I'll tell them my half. But remember, your half without my half isn't half as good."

"Guys, the family doesn't need your plan. And they don't need *you*—they've hired a new nanny," Mary told them.

"Oh, hi, Mary," Myron said, acting as if he hadn't said hello to her moments before. "What are you doing here?"

"*I'm* the Wohlfardts' new nanny," she told them. "I'm moving in this afternoon."

Then it was Martin's and Myron's turn to fall on the floor.

CHAPTER
TWENTY-EIGHT

What happened after that? You might be sorry
you asked.

Mary, in her first official act as the family's
new nanny, helped Mrs. Wohlfardt up off the
floor. Then she helped Mr. Wohlfardt off the
floor. And lastly, she helped Nathan and David
up off the floor.

Martin and Myron, however, stayed down
on the carpet. Each man began kicking and
screaming, throwing a tantrum much as a two-
year-old would.

"There, there," comforted Mrs. Wohlfardt.

"Where, where?" asked Martin.

"There, there," comforted Mr. Wohlfardt.

"Where, where?" asked Myron.

Nathan and David got down on the floor with the men, trying to get them to calm down and stop crying.

It worked.

A few minutes later, the five adults and two boys all met for hot cocoa in the kitchen.

"They're having hot cocoa," David whispered to his brother.

"I can see and hear that this time," Nathan told him.

Knowing that his whipped-cream presentation hadn't solved the two-nanny problem weeks before, Mr. Wohlfardt tried an entirely different approach with the three nannies:

Marshmallows.

Using marshmallows in their cups of hot cocoa, Mr. Wohlfardt charted out the whole situation: two boys, three nannies.

Mrs. Wohlfardt, who didn't have much faith in her husband's food-based demonstrations, left the room. Mr. Wohlfardt thought perhaps he heard her speaking on the phone in the next room, though he knew that the way things were going, she might just be sitting alone talking to herself.

"And so, you understand," Mr. Wohlfardt said, as the three nannies nodded but clearly didn't understand, "the marshmallows represent all of you, and this cup of cocoa represents the job we have to offer. If marshmallow number 1 is Martin, and I put it in the cup—"

"I'll melt! If that marshmallow is me, I'll melt in the hot cocoa!" Martin said.

"Remember, Martin . . . the marshmallow is not *actually* you," Mr. Wohlfardt told him. "It's a marshmallow representing you."

"Whew, that's a relief," Martin said.

Mr. Wohlfardt's attempt to explain and fix the triple-nanny situation went on for a while with much delicious marshmallow eating, but without much success. Fortunately, success was about to enter from the next room, because Mrs. Wohlfardt came back with especially good news for all.

"Hmm, perhaps if we tried it with *mini*-marshmallows," Mr. Wohlfardt was saying as his wife gleefully interrupted him.

"I did it, I did it, I did it," Mrs. Wohlfardt said.

"Congratulations! I knew you could do it!" Mr. Wohlfardt said, thrilled to be interrupted and tossing the bags of marshmallows

and mini-marshmallows aside. "What did you do?"

"I solved the whole problem! For you! For me! For Nathan! For David! For Martin! For Myron! For Mary!" Mrs. Wohlfardt boasted.

"Do tell," Mr. Wohlfardt begged. "Do tell."

"Well, I was in the den and I was thinking, 'What do people want more than anything?' " Mrs. Wohlfardt said.

"Socks you never have to wash?" Myron guessed.

"A lifetime supply of ketchup-covered pretzels?" Martin guessed.

"Good guesses, but you're both wrong, Myron and Martin," Mrs. Wohlfardt told them.

She went on to explain that she was thinking that what everyone wants more than anything is a reliable, responsible caregiver for themselves and their loved ones. Martin said that would have been his next guess.

"So," Mrs. Wohlfardt told the group, "I called some neighbors and asked if they'd want to know about some highly recommended, kindhearted professionals."

"Do you mean *us*?" Myron wanted to know.

"Indeed I do," Mrs. Wohlfardt said. "And indeed they did."

"Really?" Mr. Wohlfardt asked, wide-eyed.

"Really," Mrs. Wohlfardt said. "The Kendall family needs help watching their son, Beckett."

"The Kendall family? Ooh, I love their itty-bitty kitty!" Martin said.

"Yes, I remember," said Mrs. Wohlfardt. "And the Clarks have baby triplets and could definitely use daily assistance."

"The Clarks? Such a clean lawn!" Myron said, though only Nathan and David knew what he meant.

"Plus, that nice elderly lady Mildred Williams who recently moved to town needs an aide to help her when she goes shopping for piano music," Mrs. Wohlfardt added.

"What does all that have to do with us?" Mary wanted to know.

"I'm glad you asked," Mrs. Wohlfardt said. "After I got off the phone, I knew I needed a plan, so I started to dabble. . . ."

Mr. Wohlfardt nodded cheerily. He liked hearing that, especially the word "dabble."

Mrs. Wohlfardt then outlined a schedule in which the three nannies could share the responsibilities at the Wohlfardt house, the Kendall house, the Clark house, and Mrs. Williams's cottage. They could rotate responsibilities, so none of them would get bored, and each family would get the help they needed while sharing the nannies' S-A-L-A-R-I-E-S.

"Brilliant! It's the best of all possible worlds!" Mr. Wohlfardt said.

"I like it!" said Martin.

"I like it!" said Myron.

"I like it!" said Mary.

"And adding to the terrificness," Mrs. Wohlfardt said, not really knowing if that was a word, "you'll see each other—and our boys—daily!"

"Bravo!" Mr. Wohlfardt cheered.

Then suddenly he frowned.

"But, dear," Mr. Wohlfardt said, "if they're all working in different homes, how will they see each other daily?"

"When they all come home each night to sleep," Mrs. Wohlfardt said. *"Right here in our house."*

That's when Mr. Wohlfardt once again fell to the floor. Good thing his head landed on the bags of marshmallows. And, of course, mini-marshmallows.

Everyone loves a neat, tidy, happy ending, and it seems that the Wohlfardt family and their three (!) nannies had one. Until . . .

. . . the doorbell rang.

Mrs. Wohlfardt, thinking it was one of the Kendalls, or a Clark, or Mildred Williams, gleefully opened the door. What she saw and heard next was perhaps the very last thing in the world she was expecting.

It was a young woman who was the spitting image of Mary Huron Delp (without the spit).

She said, "Hello, my name is Maureen Heller Duggan. I'm here for the nanny job. . . ."

"SISTER!" Martin yelled.

"SISTER!" Myron yelled.

"SISTER!" Mary yelled.

"OH, BROTHER!" all four Wohlfardts yelled.

As a print and television writer, Alan Katz has majored in silliness for more than thirty years. He's written for a whole bunch of Emmy-nominated TV shows, animated series, award shows, and a slew of Nickelodeon projects. He is also the author of many illustrated books of poems for kids, such as *Take Me Out of the Bathtub and Other Silly Dilly Songs*. He lives in Connecticut with his family, including his twin sons.

www.alankatzbooks.com

Kris Easler has a master's degree in illustration from Savannah College of Art and Design and lives in Chicago, Illinois.

www.kriseasler.com